Memoirs of a Crazed Mind

Harry Carpenter

Dedicated to Audrey, who puts up with all my crazy.

"*I met him, fifteen years ago. I was told there was nothing left. No reason, no conscience, no understanding; even the most rudimentary sense of life or death, good or evil, right or wrong. I met this six-year-old child, with this blank, pale, emotionless face and, the blackest eyes... the *devil's* eyes. I spent eight years trying to reach him, and then another seven trying to keep him locked up because I realized what was living behind that boy's eyes was purely and simply... *evil*.*"

-Doctor Loomis

Introduction

The following is a transcription of tapes from Doctor Margaret Sanchez, found in an abandoned box located in the crawlspace of a townhome. Some of the tapes were damaged during the storage process. There were no visible dates or times on the tapes. They are not an official transcription written from a certified transcriber, so the official formatting may be off. What follows may be traumatic, jarring and disturbing.

You have been warned.

Chapter 1

Entry 100

Jesus fuck. Where do I even begin, Maggie? You want childhood? I guess we can always start there. Is this thing recording? Do the batteries even work? Test. Test. One...two. Ok. I think we are good to go here. I'm only telling this shit one time, Marge. It always hurts to talk about the past. Does anyone ever have a good childhood? Are they all rainbows and sunshine, and I got shit and rotten? You're the doc, you tell me. Should I start at the very beginnings? Ok, well, I started as sperm in my father's nut sack. Too far back? Ok, ok. Lighten up.

ΔΔΔ

It all started way back when I was a kid. The '70s were a hell of a time to be alive. Love on every corner. Drugs on every street. I didn't give a shit about any of that. I was five years old, a product of the free love of the '60s. I was an only child. My mother regretted not having more children and probably still does to this day. Things might have been different if I had a little brother or sister. At five years old, it's hard to tell something is off with a kid,

9

ya know? We are all just goofy, pretending we are astronauts and shit. I always wanted to be a cowboy. I loved watching John Wayne flicks. I wished I lived in the west.

I think I was normal for a while. At least, your clinical definition of what you call '*normal.*' As I grew up, I had a few friends on my block and watched television like every other kid. We played outside. We'd ride our bikes out to a creek or other landmark and waste the daylight hours. I'd like to think we were doing all of the right things. I had a friend, Johnny. This kid was a little shit. A delinquent little bastard, but he was my best friend. His dad was some war hero and let us play with his knives all the time. I didn't really get it at the time, but that guy was really fucked up.

I can think back to one time, me and Johnny were in the basement playing with some knife his pop gave us to mess with. We were practicing opening and closing it like they do in the movies. I wanted to know how to flip it around like a badass. Johnny got close, but he'd always cut the shit out of his hand every time. We'd watch his dad to it all the time. He'd just stare at the wall, flipping the butterfly knife open and closed. He'd never even look at it either. We wanted to be that cool. I wanted to be like that guy. My dad split when I was just a baby, so this guy was the closest I'd have to a real dad.

My mom would always blame me for the reason Dad left. She'd nag me all of the time. Apparently, I was a difficult birth, and it was a disaster in that hospital room. Dad couldn't hang and left Mom at the hospital. I ain't seen him since then. Hell, I didn't even see him that day. She said he was waiting in the hospital waiting room and just wasn't there anymore. That chickenshit just split and left my mom in the O.R. as they patched her back together. She wasn't the same after that.

So anyways, me and Johnny were hanging out down by the creek one day. I loved being down there. It was quiet. The only sounds you heard were the splashing of water over rocks and some bugs. There were some frogs, usually if it just rained the day before.

Johnny brought over some cat he found, hiding in the woods nearby. He held it by the neck, and it wriggled and screeched to get loose. Every time the cat would try to break free, Johnny would tighten the grip around its neck. He walked over to me.

"Hey, you want to see what's inside this cat?" Johnny asked as he reached for his knife in his pocket.

I sat there quietly. I didn't say a single word. My heart was racing. I could feel my pulse inside the temples of my head. I felt like my world was a haze, but I was there the whole time. Johnny whipped out the knife and played with the blade in one hand for a moment. We started to figure out how to get the technique down. The cat wriggled again, this time scratching his face. Johnny let his grip go.

"You asshole! You're dead, cat!" He yelled as he gripped his knife and began to chase the cat.

It was an orange housecat. I could tell he belonged to someone since it had a collar.

ΔΔΔ

Ok, I'll stop right there, Doc. I like cats. I had a bunch of em growing up. I had one at my last apartment. It was a stray that I took in. Some black and white cat. I wasn't too keen on killing animals. I know you guys always profile people like me and assume we grow up with mommy issues. We are nothing but animal killers and squirrel torturers, but that ain't true, is it? You guys can't really peg people that did something like this, can ya?

I think what upsets me more is that you all think you got it figured out. You got the motive, the victim, the method. You got it all locked down. Ain't no question in your mind that you're possibly wrong. The science says it's right. Them other doctors, FBI guys, and the assholes that study me all got it right. Wrong.

11

ΔΔΔ

I followed Johnny through the creek. He was splashing like crazy, giving chase to this cat. I managed to catch up to him as he grabbed the cat one more time. He pulled the blade out once more and placed the cat against a tree.

"You stupid shit! I got all wet! Stupid cat!" Johnny screamed at the cat.

The cat howled and wailed as he held its throat against the tree. The back legs kicking and scratching him, drawing blood with each kick. He didn't seem to care.

"Ok, let it go, man," I calmly said. He had a knife in his hand, after all.

"Hold its back legs. It keeps kicking me, and it's pissing me off!" Johnny said to me.

I hesitantly reached up to grab the legs. I looked into the cat's eyes. That's where it went all downhill for me. It was just someone's cat. He wasn't bothering nobody out here. Probably just chasing frogs or something.

"Stop!" I screamed out to Johnny.

Something snapped in me. I felt so much adrenaline. I shoved Johnny away from the cat. He immediately loosened his grip, and the cat tore off into the woods. I looked down at my hands. They were covered in blood. The cat wasn't cut, was it? I looked over at Johnny, ready to deal with his attitude. I assumed we were going to fight.

He was laying down over a large rock nearby. I probably pushed him too hard.

"Stop foolin', Johnny," I called to him.

He didn't move.

"Ok. It's not funny anymore."

12

No motion came from him. Blood flowed through the water from where he lay. I calmly walked over to him and rolled him over. He had stab wounds all to his face, hands, and body. I couldn't count how many there were. His head was crushed a bit, I assume by the rock. I immediately dropped his body.

"Shit, shit, shit!" I called out, looking around to see if anyone was nearby.

I had to think of something. I was still gripping my knife. I washed the blade off in the water of the creek and put it back in my pocket. I thought about hiding him in the woods somewhere. Most people would probably tell their parents or get the cops. I was looking for a way out of this to not get caught. It clicked in my head after about ten minutes of panic; *The bicycle.*

I decided to hoist Johnny up onto my bike, letting his head rest on my handlebars. I climbed on behind him. We rode down on one bike as it was since he had a flat tire. We are leaving almost the same way we showed up. I peddled carefully up the hill. I made sure to make it appear that it was just two boys sharing a bike together on a Sunday afternoon. My mind raced. I didn't know exactly where to go. I didn't know who to tell or what to do. I figured it was best to get to Johnny's house.

I pedaled as hard as I could. We lived in a busy neighborhood, full of rowhomes. Someone was bound to see. They'd see... unless I was riding hard and fast enough. I pushed all the way up Main Street. I took as many side streets and alleyways I could to stay out of sight. I needed to get somewhere to think. I don't even know if anyone saw us as we rode back to his house, but Johnny was still not moving.

I rolled up to Johnny's house and dropped my bike in the yard. The bicycle and Johnny hit the ground with a loud 'thud.' My heart didn't race as much as before. My vision wasn't blurred. I was focused. I needed to figure this out. I grabbed him by the hand and pulled his limp body over my shoulders. I fumbled with the back door as I balanced his body on my shoulder. The backdoor was unlocked. It swung open with an audible squeal. I pulled us both into the house and carefully closed the door.

I looked around the kitchen. There were paper towels on the countertop. I grabbed a wad of them and tried to put them under Johnny to stop some of the blood from staining the house. I pulled him forward through the kitchen. Thankfully, the basement door was straight ahead. I could hear his dad watching something on the television. I wasn't about to get caught now. I pulled his body to the stairs, and with one hard tug, his body went tumbling.

"The hell are you two faggots doing?" Johnny's father yelled.

"Sorry! We were playing! We will be quiet!" I hollered back to him.

I didn't hear any floorboards creak. Johnny's dad didn't get up from the chair. He was probably too drunk to care. He just wanted to know what the noise was. With Johnny at the bottom of the stairs, I began to think. I wasn't as panicked as I was when it happened. Did I stab Johnny? All at once, it flashed back to me. I had grabbed his hand that held the orange cat and plunged my knife into his side. The cat was let go and ran off. He must have punched me because I had a painful swelling above my right eye. Another vision swept over, as I was holding his head and smashing it against the rock I found him upon.

I rested my body against the wall. I didn't know what else to do. I cried. I laughed. All at once, everything dried up. I had no more laughter. I shed no more tears. I was in planning mode. I grabbed Johnny by the arm and pulled him over to a large rocking chair in the central part of the room. I set him up in the chair. He kept slouching and sliding out. That was pissing me off. I looked around his father's tools for anything that could help.

I managed to find some bungee cords and rope in the tool room. I went back to Johnny and sat him back up. I used the bungee cords to hold his torso up. I tied his hands and feet to the

14

chair, so he'd stop sliding. I used one more rope to hold his head up, so he didn't lean too far forward and fall out. I needed time to think about what happened. I decided to use the rest of the paper towels to clean the blood off the floor. I must have been cleaning for hours.

By the time I looked up, it was raining outside. Part of me thought about staying the night, and the other part of me thought about riding my bike home in the storm. The rain never bothered me. My mom was probably going to kill me if I didn't tell her where I was, not that she really cared anyhow. It was just the default parent mode kicking in probably. She didn't actually worry about me. She didn't even know who half my friends were. Any reasonable parent would have a bit of concern for their kids, even though most of us were allowed to run around freely all day until the streetlights kicked on.

I decided I'd call my mother. I dialed the house number and waited for it to ring. The phone rang several times before she picked up.

"Hello?" she asked as she answered the phone.

"Mom, can I stay the night at Johnny's? The storm is bad." I said as innocently as possible.

There was a pause over the phone for a moment, followed by an audible sigh.

"Fine. I don't give a shit. I'll just throw your dinner away then," Ma said as she hung up the phone.

I probably didn't even have dinner.

I went to bed, hungry. I laid on the floor near Johnny, with only a small dusty blanket covering me. I don't think I'd had a better night's sleep, considering I was on a cold tile floor with a thin sheet. I didn't dream, but I know I slept hard. It was morning before I knew it.

I crept up the stairs, saying goodbye to Johnny as I left. I told him I'd see him tomorrow. I went through the back door and picked up my bike. I shook some of the rainwater out of the bike and rode it straight home. I thought I saw the orange cat a few times on the bike ride back, but it was probably just my eyes playing tricks on me.

I slammed my bike down in the front yard and went into the house. My mother was in the kitchen. I could tell because the cigarette smoke was strongest there.

"Have fun?" she asked.

I wasn't sure if she was being a smart ass or was genuinely concerned where the hell I was. I shrugged and headed up to my room. I laid on my back, staring up at the ceiling of my bedroom. I wasn't thinking about anything. Everything was just a blank. I didn't think about what happened yesterday, nor did I think about anything else of consequence. I just laid there, motionless. A smile came over my face, however. I was thinking about the little orange cat. He was going to be okay.

∆∆∆

I probably visited Johnny a few times throughout the week. It was a great summer vacation from school. Eventually, school started back up, and Johnny didn't show up to school. The principal, teachers, and a few other parents got really worried. They sent some cops to check the house. Johnny's dad was passed out drunk that day, so I heard. They came in, and he drunkenly pointed to search the house. The cops apparently went to Johnny's room, and it was empty. He wasn't there. The room had some dust on the blankets, desk, and some things that should have been actively used by a kid in their room.

They fanned out and checked the basement. I heard one of the parents at the school tell another one that the body was so disgusting looking that one of the cops resigned. I didn't know what that meant at the time. They cuffed Johnny's dad, and he's still in jail, or at least he was if he didn't die already. They said he was "Shell Shocked" from the war and probably killed his kid. I didn't say a word. His dad was a piece of shit anyway. All he did was watch tv and lay around. Just because you got one leg, don't mean you should just lie around all day. But you probably don't care about him. You're here for my stories, right? I need to get a drink of water before the next one.

Chapter 2

Entry 101

This thing back on? I guess that's what the red light means. Recording. Well, we got my childhood out of the way. Nothing much really happened for a little while. At least, not until I started dating. My teenage years weren't nothing too eventful. I kept going to school and getting decent grades. I didn't really even think about Johnny until we started bringing it up today. The teachers loved me. I wasn't the smartest kid, but I got by just fine.

By the time I was fifteen, I had started working at some gas station down the road from me. I'd been in there buying a pop once a day, so the owner thought I should just work there. It wasn't bad to have a few bucks in my pocket, either. I worked the late shift. I didn't have no problem going to school during the day, only to turn around and work until four in the morning. Didn't bother me none much at all. Not like I slept anyhow. There some kind of psycho mumbo jumbo you can stick with that? Not sleeping? I don't even know, Midge. Seems like that's something we should be looking into.

Chapter 2

Late one night, I was working alone at the gas and dime shop. I think it was a Tuesday or a Wednesday. Must have been, oh, ten or eleven-thirty at night. I was mopping the floor back by the chips. I remember this night so well. It almost plays in my head during my dreams, when I do actually sleep. I had my stupid nametag attached to my stupid collared shirt on. Green and yellow were the colors, and I hated it. I made do with it, though.

I heard the front doorbell jingle. I glanced up at the security mirror up on the wall. Some blonde-haired girl, I'd guess she was about my age. Attractive, and in shape. Probably played some sport or was a cheerleader. I rested the mop against the wall near the freezer coolers so I could go greet her. I went to the front of the store and gave an awkward wave. I was never good with the ladies.

"Hey," I said.

"Oh, hi," the girl shyly responded. She kept looking at the magazines in front of the register.

I beat my brain to find more intelligible words to throw out of my mouth to this girl.

"Nice night, right?"

She smiled. "Yeah, I guess."

Smooth, right? I decided I'd introduce myself and slink back to my mopping duties.

After awkwardly pointing to my shirt nametag, and motioning toward my mop, I went back. Blondie knew where to find me if she was ready to check out. I started cleaning the floors once again. I glanced back in the mirrors a few times to catch a glimpse of her. She had very smooth skin. It was almost like a porcelain doll. Who comes out to the gas station this late to read some teen bop magazine? Was she really that hard-pressed to know how to tease your hair in thirty ways to drive your man wild at this hour? I put the mop back into the water to reset and move to another aisle.

The whole time I was watching her in the mirrors. I was fascinated, almost taken over by her. I realized I was putting water everywhere it shouldn't be. My boss was going to kill me since I probably ruined about fifty bucks in dry dog food bags. Maybe it wouldn't look so bad when it dried up? I couldn't very well tell him I was gawking at some eye candy at midnight instead of cleaning. I decided to go to the back and grab some towels and try to soak up the water on the food. I doubt a dog is gonna notice that it got wet at some point.

I smiled over at Blondie as I walked to the back room. She barely glanced up from the book, but I think I saw a half-smile. *Not bad, rookie. Keep it up, and you might be able to hold an intelligent conversation next time,* I thought to myself. I fumbled around to grab a roll of towels from the shelf. I must've missed hearing the doorbell chime. I returned to the sales floor to see two guys wandering the floor. I walked past the first one, not even looking in his direction. The second one was headed toward the drink coolers to grab a pop or something.

I started blotting up the extra water on the dog food. It wasn't until I started gathering up the sopping wet towels that I noticed the darker haired individual had tracked in mud from outside. He left sticky, disgusting mud footprint trails from the door all the way to the coolers. The cooler floor that I just mopped. I was pissed off. I'd never been too courageous to speak up for myself, but today was the day.

ΔΔΔ

Now, don't get me wrong, Doc. I ain't no pussy. I just never really got into confrontation. I preferred to stay clear of schoolyard fights. I didn't get into tussles with the neighborhood kids. I wasn't riding around on my bike looking for a brawl. I'm not a violent guy. I don't like to get into fisticuffs with people, not my style.

I also ain't no clean freak. Don't think I got that disease where I gotta clean everything all the time, neither. I just don't appreciate people fucking up what I just cleaned up. You understand that, right?

ΔΔΔ

Anyway, where was I? Oh, yeah. The mopping job that just got messed up. I gathered my towels and walked them to the trashcan. I pitched them inside, and they landed with a loud thud on the bottom. It must have been enough to draw attention and shake up the silence.

"Hey, you're outta Root Beer, buddy," Dark and Muddy called to me.

"Oh, yeah. Sorry."

I kept my head down. I was still pissed off about the mud trails.

"You gonna get me a drink, freak?" he called back over to me.

I didn't have any more bottles in the back. Some part of me decided I should go back there and look so I can get off the floor for a moment. I nodded my head like an idiot, moving toward the back. I'd no idea what I was doing. I started staring blankly at the shelves in the supply room. I knew there wasn't anything there, so what was I looking at?

I decided that I looked at the empty space long enough. I stepped back onto the floor. I saw the tracked in mud first. It now spanned two more aisles to include in front of the pet food. Assholes. I looked around and saw the two of them had surrounded Blondie. She looked completely uncomfortable. She came here to read about the latest celebrity gossip at midnight, not to be harassed. I crept past the trio, back to my mop. It was missing. *Where the fuck did I put my mop?*

I glanced around, hoping to spot the tip of the wooden handle from where I was standing. I swear I stuck it back into the bucket. I peered around the corner of the aisle. It didn't fall to the ground. I must be losing my mind. Did I take it to the stockroom with me? I took one last look around the aisle tops to see if I rested it against something. Dark and Muddy and his friend were still bothering Blondie. She didn't look very happy to be dealing with them. Then I saw it; my mop.

Dingleberry Dan, Dark and Muddy's friend, had grabbed a few of them condoms that were in the next aisle and started putting them over the mop handle. Now he's wasting product. I figured my boss would be pissed if he came in here at six and saw all of this had happened. I decided to walk over and say something.

"H-hey. Put that down. That's not yours," I said, as awkwardly as possible.

The two of them stopped harassing Blondie immediately. They were now focused on the hero of the day.

"You want your little mop? Here!" DD said as he hurled it at my face. The wood handle struck me in the cheek. That kinda hurt. Dark and Muddy walked around to the side of me, and backward down the aisle. He was all smiles. He raised a foot up to the lip of the bucket and tipped it over. I watched as a few gallons of water spilled down the aisle. I was practically seeing red. I didn't want to have to do more work than I had to tonight.

"Leave him alone!" Blondie yelled to the two guys. I don't know why she stuck up for me.

I felt a hand on my shoulder. I don't know what really happened after that. All I know is I grabbed the mop handle as hard as I could and thrust backward with it. After I gained the full sense of what happened, that's when it set in. I jammed the condom covered end directly into the eye socket of Dingleberry Dan. He was still alive and screaming. Blondie was screaming. Dark and

Chapter 2

Muddy was screaming as well as he came running up the aisle, slipping on the water.

I realized I wasn't screaming. I was cold and calm. I decided to start screaming frantically to join the club. Dark and Muddy stumbled his way up to me. He slipped on some of the water that was on the floor as he charged me. I grabbed him by the head and slammed it into the cash register. His body dropped to the ground. I started to pull the register from the countertop that it rested on, sliding it to the edge of the surface. It eventually hit a tipping point, dropping off the countertop and onto the head of Dark and Muddy. He immediately stopped flailing.

Dingleberry Dan still had one eye remaining. He had managed to pull the mop from the socket of his other eye, condom still dangling from the socket. I wasn't even disgusted by what I saw. His eye had been destroyed, with a flap of rubber hanging from the left corner, resting on his nose. I forgot about Blondie. I pulled out my switchblade. The very same one that Johnny gave me on the last day we spoke. I plunged it into the throat of Dingleberry Dan and pulled it to the left, hard.

I started to stab Dan a few more times before I realized that I had done what I did. I stopped. I dropped the knife and Dan. Both hit the floor.

I backed up a bit and slumped against the magazine rack. Blondie had already made her way to the phone behind the counter and dialed the police. I knew this was it. I wasn't upset that I killed someone. I was upset that I was going to jail, and my life was over. I just stared blankly at the two bodies that lay on the blue carpet in front of the cash register. I stared. I don't even remember blinking.

I must have zoned out because I was snapped back by red and blue lights out in front of the store. I didn't have time to cut and run. I figured it was best to just face the music and talk to the cops. Three officers came in, guns out. Blondie was first to throw her hands in the air from behind the register area. I guess they assumed I was a corpse because I wasn't even moving. They didn't even bother to look my direction.

My hearing and vision came back to. I could make out what the cops and Blondie were all saying. The next thing I knew, Blondie had put her hands on both of my shoulders.

"This is the guy. He saved me!" she cried to the police.

The first officer took a knee.

"Is this true, buddy? You ok?" he asked, flipping to a new page in his notebook.

I stared at him for a few minutes. I blinked to show I was in fact, alive. My mind was racing. I was thinking about what I'd have to do in prison. Could I even afford a lawyer? I'm a minor still, so I'll probably get a lighter sentence, right?

"Hey, can you stand?" the officer asked.

I nodded. Both officers each reached out an arm to assist me to my feet. I rested against the countertop, just inches from a mashed potato skull. It didn't bother me one bit. The cops didn't pay no mind to it. They probably assumed I was so shaken up that I didn't even realize what happened. I knew what happened. I felt it all. I kinda liked it, in a way. I got to be a hero.

We walked to the stock room to get us out of the carnage. The cops let me clean myself up a bit in the sink. I didn't really have any noticeable cuts or injuries, but it was hard to tell under all of that blood.

"Jesus, buddy. You ok?" the officer said as he observed what I assumed was an injury.

I looked at what he was inspecting. I had a giant gash on my side. I guess I got knifed during the struggle and didn't even notice.

"We gotta patch you up. EMT's are on the way. I guess the other guys don't need them, but we can get you some help."

I nodded and leaned back into a wooden chair next to the sink. Thank god for our low budget breakroom, right?

ΔΔΔ

I got patched up by the paramedics. I had a two-inch stab wound to my side. It just missed my kidneys. Blondie apparently gave a statement saying I was just working when the two guys attacked her, and I asked them to leave. She said they turned immediately on me and started assaulting me. They were hitting me with the broom and even stabbed me. I eventually struggled my way out on top, and obviously, they see the end result. I was a goddamn hero.

I don't even remember it that way. The crazy thing is it didn't even make the paper. It was so gruesome; the news didn't even want it. My boss came in and wanted to know why all the cops were running around. I told him Blondie's version of the story. He gave me the next few days off, with pay. He was a nice guy. I wonder whatever happened to him.

Anyways, turns out the security cameras were just for show and didn't even have tapes in em. All the cops had to go off of were me and Blondies' stories, which both lined up. I made sure I told her story too. Funny thing is, I made more of a mess in that store than those two assholes ever did with the muddy shoes.

Ok, I think I'm done for now. I gotta take a piss.

Chapter 3

Entry 102

Nothing like a good wiz to reset. So, since this thing is recording – shall we?

△△△

It musta been a few months later. Maybe a year. Who the hell knows? I lose track of time, ya know? Anyways, I ended up dating Blondie. Go figure. Something about that 'damsel in distress' and a heroic action really did it for her. I didn't think anything of it. Never really had girlfriends before. It wasn't like I was an outcast, I just enjoyed reading my books more than dealing with that bullshit. I saw too many schoolmates have broken hearts and lose their shit over some asshole or bimbo that hurt them. Not my cup of tea, honestly, but Blondie got me.

We did the usual couple things. We went to see some movies. Blondie liked that Star War one that came out about the space pirates and sword fighting with lasers. Not bad, but man, did it drag. We had just finished seeing that movie and were leaving through the exits when some asshole slammed into me with his big bag of popcorn. I was hit with at least a hundred kernels. I was pissed. The guy, we'll call him Chuckles, just laughed it up. Just sat there, yuckin' it up with his buddies. What a shit.

I shook out a few kernels from my leather jacket. I tried to look cool, even though I wasn't. I liked to wear leather for a bit. Hell, it was the eighties, who didn't like leather? Hell of a change from the bright hippie colors. Anyways, I brushed the popcorn and butter disaster off me. The butter, however, discolored my jacket. I was furious. I pushed the guy hard against the wall, ready to knock his lights out. I'm not a violent guy, but you don't put greasy shit all over another man's clothing. It's just not right. Blondie grabbed me by the bicep.

"Don't hurt him," she pleaded. Her heart didn't really sound like she was fully convinced I shouldn't rearrange his face, either.

I did as she asked. I lowered my arm and headed outside with my woman. My mind was racing. I was ready to knock that guy's teeth out over some butter. His buddies were still giggling as we left through the side doors, letting the bright streetlight just outside bleed into the room. The streets weren't too busy. For a Saturday night, the cars would usually pack the streets for a night out on the town. There was a football game across town, and most of the city was either inside watching or sitting in their cars in the parking lot to tailgate. I always thought that was stupid.

Anyways, I was ready to call it a night. I told Blondie I'd get her a cab. I hailed her the next one that came trolling the streets. I guess I got lucky. I didn't even think about the fact they were probably hovering over there by the big game.

"I had a great time! Sorry about your jacket. Call me when you get home?" she asked as she climbed into the cab.

I smiled and closed her cab door behind her. I waved her off as the cab started toward her place. I kept looking back down at the giant shiny grease stain that was probably wearing away at the material. I needed to get the jacket cleaned. How the hell do you clean a jacket, anyhows?

ΔΔΔ

I mean, seriously. I loved that jacket. That was my lady-killer jacket. The collar. The pockets. The zippers. Everything about that jacket screamed sexual tyrannosaurus. I never found another one like it. I searched the mall for a replacement after this whole ordeal; no dice. I wish we had things like the internet back then, I coulda found that jacket. I don't even know what the hell brand it was anymore. Let me say that I looked damn good, I can assure you that, Marge.

ΔΔΔ

Anyways, I waved her off and she got in the cab. Oh, yeah. That's right. I went back inside the theater to get some towels and use the sink. I was going to do my best to save this coat. I told the kid at the ticket booth that I was just inside and showed him my stub. I showed him the butter problem, and he waved me over to the bathroom. I looked as upset as I did about this mangled leather.

I went inside the latrine. I couldn't hear myself think. All the hand dryers were blowing loudly. It's enough to piss you off, you know? Well, as the dryers started to die off, I could hear again. I went to the sink and turned the knob. I figured cold water should be safe enough to begin with. I couldn't use paper towels because this place wanted to use goddamn jet engines to dry my hands. I worked with what I had. I splashed water on the jacket and used my hand to rub away the oils and grease.

While I was uselessly mixing oil and water, I heard something from the other end of the shitters. It was Popcorn Punk and his cronies. They were chuckling about something while they pissed. I didn't pay no mind at first, that is until the ginger one said something.

"I can't believe you have Lindsay meeting you here. What if Brenda finds out?"

"Fuck her. She said she had a headache and couldn't come out tonight. Besides, Lindsay has bigger tits. Sounds like I win, fellas," Popcorn Putz said.

I tried not to look over at them. I just kept my head down, brushing water and grease into the sink. They finished their group piss, shook each other's dicks, and headed back to the movie theater. Didn't even wash their hands, filthy animals. I kept scrubbing while they chuckled their way back to the cinema. The dark-haired friend had the most annoying 'stoner' laugh. You know the kind. The kind that is just deep, low, and goofy. Looking back, that cartoon with the two kids on MTV, back when it used to play music videos.

I musta been scrubbing for a half hour or more. Eventually, I gave up the dream. I used the dryer to blow extra water off the jacket and my hands and put it on. I looked in the mirror. Where there was once a beautiful black leather jacket now stood a black leather jacket with a big circle of brown discoloring. Motherfuckers.

I threw the jacket off of me and tossed it against the wall in a rage. I even tried to rip the stupid dryer off the wall. I kicked the trash can a few times before finally deciding to leave the restroom. I checked the pockets and jammed my jacket into the garbage. I'm sure some lucky schmuck is wearing a lady-killing leather jacket with a big brown stain on the front. I was pissed. I stormed out of the restroom and went back outside.

I sat on the curb for at least an hour. I muttered to myself. I couldn't tell you what I said, I couldn't remember even if I tried. My muttering was broken up by the occasional car rumbling by, but aside from that, I remained uninterrupted in my thoughts. Part of me wanted to pull out my switchblade and jam it into that dickhead's tires. I even got up and wandered through the parking lot, wondering what giant truck or sporty car was a monument to his ego. I couldn't figure it out. I half expected to see some vanity plate that said 'Stud' or other macho term to make him feel better about himself.

It was getting late. I didn't think about the fact that there was also some double feature playing tonight. That was just my luck. I get the nerve to wait around for this dill hole, and it turns out to be a three-hour endeavor. I don't think I could sit through a three-hour flick. I really don't know what I was even waiting around for. I was just hovering around this theater, lurking in the shadows like some kind of psycho, but I ain't crazy. I got a good head on my shoulders, I'll tell you that.

I started to nod off near the dumpsters when I heard a familiar sound. It was Chuckles. He had that same throaty laugh, coupled with a few bad jokes by Popcorn Putz. Jesus Christ, I wanted to just smash my face into a brick wall every time I heard that laugh. I saw the group of em. They passed by the parking lot. I guess they didn't even drive here? I mean, I didn't either, but I assumed they at least took some sort of ode to his ego here. I didn't move, I didn't budge. I watched as they passed by the parking lot.

ΔΔΔ

Now, I know you think I'm nuts. Who the hell hangs out by a dumpster for hours waiting for some guy to give him what for? I know you're processing me and analyzing me right now, Marge. I don't like that. Cut it out. Wouldn't you be pissed off if someone wrecked your jacket?

ΔΔΔ

Once they passed by, I got up from my hiding place. I followed close behind, but not too close. I wanted to see where this jackass lived and trash his home for what he did to my jacket. I tailed them through busy streets, a park, and eventually a block of rowhomes. It was lit well and had some lovely trees on the side of the road. The stairs looked well maintained. This was a wealthy neighborhood. I could smell the money.

I figured the group would split ways after we hit the first house, but they didn't. They all went inside the house. I assumed it was Popcorn Putz. He seemed like a spoiled rich kid to me. They went into the house, but not before I got one final yuk from Chuckles. The very sound of his laughter drilled into my spine. Sometimes I hear it when it's quiet at night. It was that bad.

I waited around the neighborhood for about a half-hour or so. I never really wore a watch, so I didn't know what time it was. I could only take a guess to my time. I decided I'd walk around to the back of the row. The houses didn't have street-side access, save for them gates in between the homes. Those were usually locked. I bet around back they'd have backyards and gardens and a way to look around. I rounded the block and made my way to the alley.

Once I was in the alley, I started to count the houses. They didn't label the houses from the back. I had to know how many houses it was down from the end of the block. I came upon a house that had grey cobblestone paving. There was some fancy car, maybe a Mercedes or something sitting on the parking pad. I walked past it. I considered keying the vehicle. There was a light on in the back window, maybe a kitchen or something. I crept up the stairway to the back porch. It was nice. They had some beautiful outdoor furniture, and even somewhere to set a fire. I wish I had these nice things growing up. Instead, I got shit.

I heard movement inside. It sounded like glass banging and clanging. Then I heard a loud thud. Maybe these kids killed each other? Maybe they did me a favor and rid the world of themselves? I just needed to give this guy a piece of my mind, even on his dying breath. I decided I needed to see what was going on. I peered around the corner into the large window. Inside, I could see a beautiful dining area. There was a long table, sat maybe twelve on a good day. Above hung an enormous glass chandelier. There were paintings on the walls that I could see. Deeper inside, I could see what was going on. The banging and clanging noises that I heard were identified. Popcorn Putz and his friend Chuckles had pulled out a massive case of records. They seemed like they were drinking too. That was the banging. Must have been a liquor cabinet or a cellar door.

I looked around on the porch. There wasn't much out there except for a few chairs, an ugly green rug, and that firepit. I decided to sit down in the chair. It was soft and quite lovely. I ended up dozing off for a few.

I woke up to the sound of a loud thud. I wasn't sure what it was. I realized I had fallen asleep outside this kid's house. I looked around to find myself still alone in the calm crisp night. It was a little cold since I ditched my jacket hours ago. It must have been one in the morning by now. They were still playing music. I again heard laughter. Particularly the laughter that burned me to the core. I don't know why I decided to hang around longer. I sat in the chair, thinking.

I don't know what I even thought about. All that I know is that when I was done my thinking, I stood up. I decided to look into the window once more. I saw Popcorn Putz, Chuckles, and the girl they were with, all over the place. They were passed out or too drunk to move the right way. One laid over some couch I could see. The other was up against a wall. The last one was stumbling through the house, heading back from the kitchen. I decided to go inside and tell them what I thought of them.

I tried the kitchen doorknob. Unlocked. I turned the knob slowly and pulled the door open. It came free with ease. I miss the days where everyone left their doors unlocked. I whirled into the kitchen and closed the door carefully behind me. The kitchen light was off, but there was plenty of illumination coming from the living area to give me light. I scanned the room a bit to see what was around. I saw a baking pan, knives, and a spoon all in the dish drainer. What the hell were these guys cooking?

I took a deep breath, cleared my head, and headed into the living room. He was going to buy me a new jacket. My mind was made up. I walked through the threshold of the door and stood in the living room. I didn't hide. I didn't lurk. I just stood still. I panned around the room. Popcorn Putz barely looked at me. Hammered beyond control. I decided to say something like, "Hey asshole, you wrecked my jacket."

Popcorn looked at me.

"Yeah? Who the fuck are you? Are you bringing us a pizza? I really want a pizza, man."

I sniffed the air. Reefer. Drinking, smoking, and probably fucking. Damn delinquents. Where the hell were their parents? My mom was at home. Why wasn't their mom? Where were the parents? Vacation, I bet. Rich people love taking those.

Chuckles started to laugh. He pointed and laughed. What the hell was so funny that it warranted a laugh? I guess the drugs will do that to you.

I walked over to him and grabbed him by the hair.

"What the fuck is so funny, clown?" I asked him.

His laughter stopped. Well, it almost finished, with a few snickers here and there to be found.

"Dude, chill. He didn't do anything to you," Popcorn shouted from the comfort of his couch.

No one bothered to move. Popcorn and crew just sat there, laughing or spacing out. What a bunch of losers. Chuckles looked at his friends, as I held his hair in my hand. He started his throaty giggle once more. From my left pocket, I pulled something out and jammed it into the throat of Chuckles. His laugh went from a throaty giggle to a bubbling gurgle. I apparently grabbed a knife from the kitchen. I took the knife out of his throat, which he immediately grasped at. I didn't go all the way through like they do in the movies. It also went right through like butter.

I'd never really stabbed someone before. This was new. The feeling of the blade puncturing the flesh. It was a unique sensation I can't describe. Maybe that feeling of pushing your finger through lunchmeat. It's a bit of resistance at first, but once you break through, you slide through like warm butter. Chuckles tried to stand up but stumbled back to the floor. It may have just been the alcohol. Fucking drunk.

The girl went to get up but staggered herself. She fell against the wall, hard. I went into the kitchen and grabbed the baking sheet. I returned to the living room, to find none of the three really moved. Popcorn's lady friend tried to get back up again. I hit her hard with the baking pan. The aluminum was thick and made a loud 'pang' sound. It was almost drowned out by the music playing on the record.

The music playing in the background almost made the act sort of a 'dance.' I would flow through to the next move at the change of the beat. I don't even remember grabbing the spoon from the kitchen, but I do remember jamming it down the throat of Popcorn Putz. I shoved it, spoon first, allowing the handle to stick out about an inch or so from his lips. He attempted to reach for it, grabbing the handle, but losing grip due to the blood that was coming from his throat. I must have hit something good.

Behind me, Chuckles tried to crawl over to the house phone just across the room. I walked over and put my boot on his neck. I pressed hard like I was trying to win a street race. I revved the engine of this make-believe car. I didn't let up until I heard an audible 'pop.' I don't think I've broken a neck before, either. I always saw it in movies, but I didn't know they were that sensitive. I'll be more careful with my own.

Once Chuckles stopped fighting back, he stopped all at once. He lies still on the floor, blood pouring from his body. I

34

wiped my boot off on the rug. Popcorn Putz gave up fighting the spoon and must have drowned in blood or suffocated. I wasn't a medical student., I had no idea how these things worked. I just knew that whatever I was doing, it was working. I wanted these assholes to feel pain. The girl didn't do much to me. These two were the ones laughing it up at the expense of my jacket.

I rested against a wall for a moment. I looked around at the devastation. There was blood everywhere. It sprayed from their bodies with everything I did. I really did a number on that brand name furniture that they had. Nobody moved. It was over. I decided to take a look around the house.

I walked upstairs and checked the bedrooms. I was right; mom and dad were away. I found their bedroom. I decided to leave it untouched. I peeked into another room just down the hall. Jackpot. I found Popcorn's bedroom. Inside, there were trophies for baseball, photos of friends, and a desk. Pretty standard room for late teens, early twenty-something. I made my way to the closet. I opened it, looking for a replacement jacket. All I found were letterman jackets and some green windbreaker. I didn't want that garbage. I walked out of the room emptyhanded and pissed off.

I sauntered back down the stairs. I was pissed. I couldn't replace my jacket. I figured I should check their pockets. I grabbed Chuckles first. His wallet was in the back pocket. I pulled it out and fished for cash. He had about twenty bucks in a variety of fives and ones. I dropped his wallet onto his body but decided to put it back into his pocket. I looked toward Popcorn. He was slumped backward over the couch. I felt around his pants for his wallet. It was in the front left pocket. He had a few more bucks than his friend. Clearly, he was the one with a proper allowance. I retrieved forty dollars and change from his wallet. I didn't replace his wallet. I threw it back at his face. It bounced off and tumbled down, stopping in between the couch cushion and his body.

I assumed the girl had a purse or something. I started to look around the room for it. As I picked through some things that were in the living room, I heard a noise. I heard some rustling. I heard stirring. I heard people.

I glanced over and noticed the girl was crawling toward the back door. Well, I should say she was trying to crawl toward the back door. I stormed over and put my foot down hard on her calf. She cried out, but it was drowned out by the music. I think it was some Ozzy or something loud. I didn't really pay any mind to the music. I had a job to do. They saw my face.

I grabbed the girl by the ankles and pulled her down towards me. I rolled her over. She had a massive gash on her face from the cookie pan earlier but was otherwise still pretty. I smiled at her. She was crying and writhing around.

"P-Please don't hurt me....Please!" she cried out.

I decided to reason with her.

"But I already hurt you. See?" I said as I pushed my fingers into the open wound on her head.

She winced and cried harder.

"You ruined my jacket. Well, you didn't, but that asshole did. Did you know Popcorn had a girlfriend?" I asked, kneeling down in front of her.

She tried to stifle her sniffles as best she could.

"I-I-Yeah. She's my best friend, but she didn't deserve him."

I remember sighing really hard. I closed my eyes for a moment, squishing my eyelids tight until I saw stars.

"Jesus Christ. At least you could have the decency to tell your friend," I said, opening my eyes again.

She crawled to put her back against the wall. She was still crying, but not as hard as before.

"I-I-I will. I promise. I'll tell her that we were together. I'll tell her everything! I'll be a good friend. Promise! P-Please!" she cried.

"No, you won't. You won't tell. She'll find out about *you guys,* though."

I said what I assumed was the boldest thing I could think of just before plunging the knife into her mouth through her skull. I actually pushed with enough force to pin her to the wall. She flailed for a moment or two, then stopped. Her eyes stayed open. It's ok, she can watch if she wants.

After about an hour, I gave up looking for her purse. I figured it was best if I get the hell out of here with the sixty bucks I got. That's almost the cost of my jacket anyhow. I'll take it as a win. I reset the record and let it play through as I walked out of the house through the back door. I left the door wide open as I went.

ΔΔΔ

I remember getting back to my house and crying for like an hour. I don't know what the hell I cried for. I had to get rid of my clothes too. I was coated in blood. I didn't even realize how crazy I looked. I had to toss my nice shoes, slacks, and my shirt. All of it was coated in sticky blood. I ended up just leaving it in a bag in the basement of my house. Hell, it's probably still there or got thrown out.

I think I cried because I had to lose my jacket and my good clothes. I think that was one of the last times I tried to dress to impress while going out.

I'm gonna need a minute, Peggy. I'm gonna mourn again for my jacket before the next sesh.

Chapter 4

Entry 103

Sometimes clothing can mean a lot to someone. I've seen some ladies lose their absolute shit over a pair of shoes at the shopping mall before. It amazes me that someone can pay hundreds of dollars for a pair of the latest shoes just because some sports star wears them. At least a jacket was practical, ya know? I was able to wear it and stay warm, enjoying all of its benefits. I could tell the difference between my jacket and every other piece of garbage on the rack.

Enough about the jacket, though. I don't think you really want to hear my wardrobe woes. I bet you're ready for the next slice of my story. Mom.

ΔΔΔ

I already told you how my childhood was. Cigarette smoked filled rooms, coupled with the blissful ignorance of being ignorant. That summed up my childhood in a nutshell. I lived with Ma until I was a man. I think it feels like centuries ago, but no human lives that long. I was in my late teens. I mighta been eighteen, nineteen years old. Blondie and me were taking a break. She thought about going off to college in another state, and I wasn't. She told me we were gonna be ok, and she would come back and we can try again. I was stupid for thinking she'd come back to me. I was an idiot for believing that fairy tale bullshit for one second.

Once Blondie stepped out of the picture, I was left working at my dead-end job with nothing. I had just graduated from high school. It was the mid-eighties. If you weren't in some fancy office building or pumping gas at the local corner store, you didn't have a job. I was lucky to have the latter. I always thought myself to be stupider than I let on, even to myself. I didn't feel much for my thinking capabilities or my trains of thought. That was probably psychosomatic and brought on by Ma. The more I distanced myself from her, the more I realized I didn't have a learning disability.

I think it was spring. I couldn't tell you what month, but it was raining. A lot. I was up in my room, listening to an albums I had just picked up from the store on my way to work one day. Some band called "Ratt." They just hit the streets, and I was digging the tunes. It wasn't until later that I grew a huge appreciation for music. I latched to the hairband tunes, of all the choices out there. They didn't call it hair metal or vintage rock back in that day, but you know what I'm talking about.

I heard a bunch of coughing. I turned up my record a bit louder. "Wanted Man" was blowing through the tiny speakers of the player, but it wasn't enough to drown out whatever was making that banging noise that was now apparent. I turned the song down. Coughing and banging sounds filled the air. I decided I'd throw on my plaid shirt, and head downstairs to see what the hell that was. I ripped open my door, and sat quietly, working to understand what that racket was. It came from downstairs. I ventured down the first flight of stairs.

I did my best to peek under the ceiling overhang that ran alongside the stairwell. I squatted down as I took the stairs to get a sneak preview of what was to come. Mother was in the living room, holding a rag to her face. The banging sound I heard was the sound of her recliner slamming back into the wall as it jumped on the floor from the coughing fits she was having. I told her smoking would be the death of her. Nasty habit, glad I never picked that one up. She never really listened to me. I usually got told to "shut the hell up" or to "know my place as a child."

She saw me coming down the stairs. She started to seize louder as the wet mucus was bouncing around in her lungs. She was paler than usual. I wasn't sure what to do. I've never been in a position to watch someone spit up blood from coughing. I wasn't a medic. I sure as hell wasn't a doctor. I walked over to the end of her recliner where her feet were raised up and stood. I didn't say a word. I stood and watched.

The napkin she used to muffle her coughs was coated in blood. I thought about giving her the courtesy of getting a new rag for her but voted against it. I felt it best to just not move. I wanted to see how this all played out. She stared at me. That was the most unsettling part. The eyes. Her dead, glossed over eyes. Her eyes were bloodshot, likely from the act of spewing up her insides the past several hours. There were flecks of yellow in the eyes as well, probably smoke-stained like the rest of the house. I don't think that's how it works, but it's what I thought at the time.

She raised a hand to reach out to me. I raised my hand and waved to her. I watched her slowly set the hand down on the arm of the chair. She seized in a coughing fit once more. This time, she didn't have the energy to raise the napkin to her mouth. Blood spewed everywhere. The front of her flowered shirt was coated in a red disaster. Those stains would never come out, I'm sure of it. I didn't do anything to comfort her. I just stood there. M.A.S.H. played on the television just behind me. I could hear the telltale sounds of its theme song pouring through the speakers. Probably some rerun marathon that she parked herself on. I never cared for that show.

I never took my eyes off Mom. She tried to get words out but was only met by a gargled mucus-filled cough. I figured I would take my moment and say my peace.

"Mother. I know you probably don't know or care. You never had. You barely knew where the hell I was on most days. I could have just vanished, and it would have done you a favor," I started, "Hell, the only time you may have noticed is if I didn't bring you a pack of smokes the next morning."

She stared at me, trying to focus on me through the smoky haze over her eyes. I doubt she could even make out my face, not that she really knew what I looked like anyhow.

"You always had a way with words, too, Mother. 'Take out the garbage you waste of life,' or 'I wish you would have been stillborn.' You always cracked me up with your witty quips."

She stared, motionless. I could see she was still with me because the light in her eyes hadn't gone out. I saw the occasional chest rise with a breath or a twitch in her eye.

"The cigarettes that you'd burn me with. The very ones I ended up buying for you at the store with the money you'd send me off with. The same ones that I purchased for you with my own money at work. The cigarettes that you'd jam into my arms every time I wronged you. Every time you felt disrespected."

She started to say something, but it only opened up another coughing fit.

"You, Mother, are an absolute piece of shit. You didn't even care what I was doing. How I was doing. You never gave a single flying shit what I did. Well, Ma, I hope you're proud."

She tried to move her hand to cover her mouth and catch some of the blood.

"I'm no doctor, but I bet you fucked your lungs up from them cigarettes. The same ones that burned me almost every afternoon. The same ones I purchased. Those death sticks are burning you right now."

She attempted to shift her body away from me but failed. I remained planted at the foot of the chair. I felt almost nothing except mild rage at bringing up old memories. Everything inside of me wanted to pour out into her lap and let her know what has been going on.

"Because of you, Johnny died. Because of you, some asshole that ruined my jacket died. Some kids died at work. It's your fault, Ma."

I stopped for a moment. I decided to walk to the kitchen and grab a Coke from the fridge. I returned, popping the can as I walked back.

"Take that back. I don't blame you. You couldn't have possibly been the reason for all of that, because there isn't a fucking thing you've ever done for me! I'd rather not even give you credit," I said as I sipped a bit of the soda.

Her eyes darted around a bit. I think I saw a tear, or that could have been her dead eyes just trying to hydrate themselves and wash some of the shit out of them. Who knows? She began to cough once again. This time, it was a bit more disgusting. A heap of blood bubbled out of her mouth and her nose.

"You were a waste of a parent. If I had someone else, I would have been better. But I'm gonna be better than that, Ma. I'm going to do something with my life, and there ain't shit you can say about it."

She relaxed a bit in the chair. Her coughing stopped. The cigarette she had in her free hand didn't slip out from her fingers as it dropped to the side of the chair. Even to the last moments, she had to have a smoke. Blood was flying from her face, but she needed that fix. What a fucking loser. I stood, staring at her body for a while. I wasn't quite sure what to do, exactly. I may have stood there for an hour or two, motionless, save for my sip of Coke now and then.

I decided to phone the cops. I told them I came home, and my mother had passed away. I tried to work up some sort of emotions. I realized after I started pretending, the real ones managed to find their way to the surface. They sent some people to the house and declared her dead. Based on my story of coming back in from shopping, and their ability to figure time of death, they said she'd been dead at least four to six hours at this point.

ΔΔΔ

She died doing what she loved; being a piece of shit. She sat there, smoking and watching tv like a lazy shit. At least the funeral was lovely. I didn't spend much on it. She left me some cash, but it wasn't much. Some neighbors and people in her old church pitched in. They almost made her life seem meaningful. They spoke about how nice she was when she would go to church. She would always give the kids candy and had even worked at the church for a bit. I realized what it was. They weren't her kids. They weren't her family. I kinda miss the old bitch, even today.

Chapter 5

Entry 104

After Ma kicked the can, I figured I should move on. I was maybe eighteen or nineteen by then. I worked with some lawyers to sell the shithole of a house I grew up in. Honestly, it mighta been the best thing I ever did. I know what you're saying, Midge. I can hear it. Something about it being therapeutic to put the past behind or some shit. Truth be told, I needed the cash to get through the next part of my life. Maybe part of me was wanting to leave that old life behind.

Before you go psychoanalyzing it, I'll stop you. It's not as deep as you think it is. I just needed cash. I wanted to do something different with my life.

ΔΔΔ

I decided after the estate was settled, I was done with this shit town I grew up in. I didn't get much in the way of liquidity from Ma and her assets, and honestly, the funeral took a good chunk of change from me. I didn't have much in the way of life skills, so I figured I could do one of two things; take up a trade skill or go to college.

I wasn't really good with my hands at all. I was absolute butterfingers and could barely cut a sandwich in half, let alone weld some metal together. I opted for the educated lifestyle. I didn't have a handle on what I exactly wanted to be when I grew up, but I sure as shit knew it wasn't going to be what my family had been. I wanted to be more. I didn't have any successful aunts, uncles, cousins. Nobody. Not a single one of em had made it out. I decided I was going to be the exception to the situation.

I went down to the local community college. Seemed nice. A bunch of smart kids about my age were moving around and running to classes. The school had a plethora of programs to choose from. I didn't know if I wanted to manage a business or be a scientist. All I know is I wanted to do more than work at a gas station, grabbing cigarettes for the smokers who barked out their orders to me. I sat in the waiting room, reading every motivational poster they had. Some of them were corny, but others were meaningful. They had the run of the mill verbiage such as "hang in there," or "do great things," or "shoot for the moon." The moon one had a small image of a half-assed cartoon rocket headed for the moon. That one I remember.

I remember talking to the counselor. They told me about the requirements and this and that. After we shot the shit about what career path I was headed for, they hit me with the costs. There was no way in shit I was affording that. Four grand? To hell with that. I am sure there is some state that existed that was much cheaper for tuition. Being that I didn't have an actual home anymore, I wasn't bound to stay in this shithole town any longer.

ΔΔΔ

I'm not a quitter. Don't think for a second I gave up on my life and turned tail. When I set out to do something, by God, I will do it. Before you peg me in your mind, know that I didn't give up. I just got sidetracked is all.

ΔΔΔ

I headed to the school store on my way out. It was a little shop that carried some school necessities like pens and books. I grabbed a really nice black bookbag. It seemed sturdy enough, with a hard-rubberlike bottom. I liked it. I took it home and stuffed it full of clothing and whatever little possessions I owned. When I say home, I mean the breakroom of the gas station that I had been sleeping in between shifts. I showed up, shoved my shit into a bag, and quit. I didn't offer an explanation. I didn't say I was headed on a soul-searching journey. I just up and left. I hit the road and didn't look back.

I thought long and hard as I walked. I wasn't sure how far I planned on walking. I didn't have a car, so walking was the only option. I didn't even have a driver's license. I figured the best choice for me would be to take the first bus out of town, and where it stops, nobody knows. I started walking in the direction of the bus station. I figured that's a good start for anyone who wants to get the hell out of their dump of a town.

Along the way, I processed some of my thoughts. I pondered over what would become of Blondie if she came back to town and couldn't find me? How would the gas station function without me, their model employee? I pushed all of my thinking to the back of my mind and kept walking along. It was getting to be dusk, so I moved a little faster to get to the station in time for what I assumed was the last bus. I'd never left town before. I hadn't so much as really ventured to the neighboring counties. I remember the wind picked up a bit, and I pushed my way on to the bus station. I needed to get the hell out of this town.

I came up to the station. It was getting late, so I wasn't hopeful of getting too far for cheap. The lady behind the counter was nice. She was extremely friendly and kept calling me Sugar Pie. I don't know if that was because of my dashing good looks that I do not possess, or as her generic term of endearment. Either way, it

46

was enough that I remembered it all these years. I asked her for the first bus out of here. I didn't care where I was going. I had a backpack full of belongings, cash in my hand, and that's all I needed. I guess she could see the look in my eyes. I was a kid that was desperate to start over.

She quickly looked through her schedule. Helen, or whatever her name was, gave a few reactive eyebrow raises to some locations. After a while, Ethyl found one. She let out a confident 'aha!' After some rustling around with her system, she produced me a bus ticket.

"Forty-three dollars, Sugar Pie," she said through the microphone.

I smiled back at her and slid the money under the window. After a few moments, she finished our transaction and pushed back a ticket. I grabbed it, happy to be out of this town. I walked away from the booth, gripping my ticket in hand. I forgot to even look at it. I was too preoccupied with leaving, that I failed to see where it was that I was moving to.

"Florida."

I didn't even realize I said it out loud so dismissive. Florida. I guess the fact I said it out loud made it real. I was getting out of here.

I boarded the bus. It was cramped and smelled like old sweat. I guess I couldn't be too picky, ya know? Anyways, I found a seat next to some older lady. She was already asleep against the window, maybe dead. The only reason I knew she was still alive was the audible whistling of her nose as she breathed. Even over the rumbles of the bus, I could hear it. Each rise of her chest. Each fall. Like a slide whistle from hell. It was going to be a long ride to Florida.

I nodded off at some point on the ride. Maybe the rumble of the bus lulled me. I was woken up by one of the other passengers. We had apparently stopped somewhere along the way to piss and stretch. I decided to get some air, as recommended by the good Samaritan who woke me. Whistles was woken up as well. The nose orchestra came to an intermission for now. I slumped off the bus, cracking my neck and back as I moved.

The air outside felt humid. I'd never felt the air with that much heat in it, or moisture. I was wearing a light jacket and decided to tie that around my waist. Compared to where I lived, this was much warmer. People milled around the area, mostly hovering around the vending machines to grab snacks and sweets. I didn't really care to do any of that. I just wandered around the building and the grounds.

It was dark out. I don't even know how long we were on that bus. I just knew it was warm and late. I had a bit of sweat starting to bead up on my brow. The air felt super thick. I was getting irritated by it. I shook it off and headed around the next corner of the building. I heard a familiar sound. The repetitive pattern of a slide whistle. "Wheeze. Whish. Wheeze. Whish." It was back. The nose orchestra was in session, and the band was tuning up.

I looked around a bit. I couldn't quite find the source of the noise. It grew louder and louder by the second. It was deafening at this point!

ΔΔΔ

Listen, Marge. I don't know if you've ever been sitting in a room where someone taps their foot like crazy, or drums on a desk. None of that compares to the wind section of the symphony of nose noise that I was audience to. This was horrible. I wouldn't put my worst enemy in my shoes.

I know it sounds petty, but goddammit, it bugged me.

ΔΔΔ

I finally rounded a small nook in the building to find whistles tucked in, resting against the wall. I waved to her as innocently as I could. She barely smiled at me. She almost curled her lip as if in protest of me finding her hiding space. We were still in earshot of the bus driver if he called to board the bus. I just stared at her, and she back at me.

"You little shits always think you deserve the world. My grandson is just like you. A spoiled shit. Where did your parents send you off this time? The islands? The Keys?" She crowed, "Entitled shits."

I don't know what happened. Looking back, I still don't know. All I do know is that the palm of my hand was placed somewhere under her bony old lady ribcage. I pressed hard. Her nose whistled more. I didn't release my grip. I pushed her into the building as hard as I could. I never took my eyes off of hers.

"My parents didn't send me anywhere, you bitch. My mother is dead. She is dead, and you'll be too."

I gave her an empty threat. I figured it would be enough to put the fear of God into her, at least. I was about to release my grip on her when something crazy happened. She gasped once or twice, and a trickle of blood came from her left nostril. I watched as the light in her eyes drifted off into the distance, almost fading away. I let my grip go immediately. *What the fuck did I do?*

Once my hand was off of her blouse, she slowly rocked to the left, finally resting against the drainpipe she tucked beside for sanctuary. I looked around quickly, realizing that no one else decided to wander much further than the restrooms and snacks. I straightened myself back up, and even adjusted Old Lady Whistler. She rested perfectly against the drain pipe. I walked around to the other side of the building. There was less lighting from the floodlights on that side.

I managed to slink into the men's room and take a quick piss. One of the older guys came in behind me after a second or two and took the urinal right next to me. I was already uncomfortable with this. Wouldn't you know it? He made small talk.

"Warm today, ain't it?" He asked.

I ignored him.

"I'm excited to get back on the road. I'm headed back to see my family. The name's D-"

"I don't care."

I cut him off. I'm taking a piss, and I don't care to make friends. If he wants to make friends with his other riding buddies, that's on him. They can have bigger dick contests to their heart's content. That's not my thing.

I finished using the restroom, washed my hands, and headed outside. D wasn't far behind. Once I threw my paper towel into the garbage, I heard a saddened scream. I perked my ears up to listen to what was going on.

"Oh, my Gawd! She's dead!"

I heard several people screaming the same thing over and over. Once I stepped into the light to join the crowd, I realized what they meant. One of the tough guys came over to me and started poking me in the chest. He wasn't being too nice about it either.

"Where the hell were you, buddy?" He asked as he jammed his fat sausage finger into my ribcage.

I felt my sweat run cold on my head. I figured this was it. He saw me go around the corner and saw what I did.

"He was taking a piss with me, guy," D chimed in.

There was a bit of rumbling from the group, but they had no reason to doubt D. We did both just emerge from the bathroom if anyone was paying attention after all. The crowd started to disperse after D stood up for me. Kudos to that guy. You'd be amazed at how many people are willing to step up for others in a time of need.

One of the ladies on the bus was a registered nurse or something. She was over with Mrs. Whistle while we formed an angry mob. She walked around the corner to disclose what she determined.

"I think she had a blood clot or something. It's a shame, really. She must have been standing back there, and just went quietly, poor thing," Nurse said, "She had bruises all over her body. It's no surprise that she had some sort of blood issue.

Bruises all over her body, she says. It really is a shame that she died of natural causes. The bus driver phoned the authorities, and we waited for them to show. We were allowed to board the bus in the meantime. Some of us went into the bus and relaxed in our chairs. I now had a window seat and more room to spread out. There weren't too many empty seats to be found, so I had the privilege of being one of the few who could spread out.

ΔΔΔ

I'm not gonna lie. After the bus company took care of everything and we hit the road, it was the most relaxing bus trip ever. Do you know what it's like to spread across two seats and be able to relax? It's a luxury, Peggy. A gift from the gods. I slept the rest of the way there and didn't regain consciousness until we saw palm trees in the morning. It was a paradise. It was gorgeous. I'd never seen anything like it.

I think I need to stretch for a few. Sitting still for too long ain't good for nobody.

Chapter 6

Entry 105

Honestly, this has been nice. Getting to tell you how I feel. Laying it all out there for you to hear. Feels good. Did I tell you about the time I got in college down in Florida? No? Get ready.

ΔΔΔ

I stuck around the point that I was dropped off by the bus for a few months. I drifted around. I didn't really have a home to speak of. I just stayed where I could. I decided I'd take my hand at school again. I was sick of living on the streets, and I probably qualified for free money from the government or something. I went down to some university that was a mile or two from the area I'd frequented. I gave up too quickly the first time around. I wanted to do something better for myself.

I went straight into the admissions office. I didn't play around. I went right in. I talked to the guy for at least an hour before we got down to the money. There ain't no financial aid out there for me, he says. How does a guy that's homeless, young, and ready to learn not to find a way into school? I stepped out of his office. I was furious. I didn't know what to do with my life. I couldn't go back home, I worked too hard to get where I was. I ran my fingers through my hair in frustration. Someone in the room felt my frustrations.

"You havin' some problems there, my friend?" a powerful voice asked from across the room.

I shrugged unassumingly. I didn't know who said it, or what they were getting at.

"No money."

A guy in a green Army uniform stepped out from the other side of the room. He was partially obscured by the pillar that separated us. The disembodied voice now had a face.

"You ever think about working for Uncle Sam? That'll pay the bills, and then some. You could serve your country, and it could serve you," he said.

He continued to approach me. He was sizing me up with his eyes, and I could feel it. I never did consider myself cut out for the service. I'm not a muscular guy, and I don't have a violent bone in my body. I couldn't bring myself to shoot some people in Iran. I saw the news. I knew we were always at war. Vietnam. Korea. Now some shit is stirring over there in the Middle East. I figured they needed people to go over there. I didn't even think about the fact these assholes always creep around campuses. I always stayed away from the shopping centers they were set up in. They even had a booth at the mall, across from the arcade.

"Never thought me much of an Army guy, to be honest. Not much soldier material to be found here," I said back, hoping to deter him.

He extended his hand out for a shake.

"Me neither. But nine years later, I'm still doing it. The name is Sergeant F—"

"I'm not cut out for this type of work. Runnin and gunnin, jumping out of planes," I interrupted.

He laughed. It was a hearty, legitimate laugh. I almost let my guard down and became a people person for a second.

"I can assure you, my friend. This isn't what it's all about! We have a ton of cool jobs you can choose from. Radios? You like those? We got those. Maps? You can read maps!"

He was really trying his hardest to sell me on the concept. I was almost buying it. Let's just say I had my fingers on the edge of my wallet. I wasn't entirely sold yet.

"I can drive. You need guys that do that?" I asked.

He smiled and became overly excited.

"Tanks, trucks, jeeps. You name it, we drive it! 88 Mike, eh? We could use more of you guys."

I didn't know what the hell he was talking about. Gibberish and jargon to me. He sounded enthusiastic. I wanted to do more with my life, so what the hell? Let's give it a whirl.

"Ok, Sarge. How do we do this thing? Give me the shortest trial period you can."

He smiled and shook my hand. I pulled my hand back, which contained a business card now. It was the recruiter's station.

"Tuesday. Come see me, say, twelve hundred? Noon? We'll do lunch and get you squared away with paperwork," Sergeant F said.

He turned and walked off back to his post. I assumed ready to recruit the next sucker. I wasn't no sucker. I was going to make this work for me.

Chapter 6

I tell you, getting a job is the hardest thing I've ever had to do in my life. I worked at that gas station for so long I didn't know how to do much else. I didn't have any people skills, social ability, or nothing. Peggy, have you ever had a problem with getting jobs doing things other than psychologically profiling people like me? Ever surf? Work in an office answering phones? I couldn't do that shit. It's not me. It's not what I want to do.

ΔΔΔ

A few days went by, and I went down to the office. 'Noon Hundred' or whatever it was called. I waited outside the station for a bit. I wanted to see who was coming and going. I didn't see much traffic coming out of the office. It must not be a busy time for em. I gripped the door handle. I looked at the poster in the window that said, 'Be All You Can Be!' *Was that me?* I was gonna be all I could? Was this what I could do?

"You comin' in or you lettin' the air out on purpose?" a voice echoed from across the room.

I stepped in and closed the door. The grumpy soldier went back to reading his paper. Everyone was kicked back and relaxing. Hell, if this was the Army life, sign me up! Can I get paid to read the paper and sit here? I can't see myself having issue with this. Before I was truly able to fully take in the surroundings, Sergeant F approached me from the left side office.

"Hey man, come on over. Let's chat."

I walked with him, oblivious to what I was getting myself into. He fed me some mumbo jumbo about serving this great country. After that, he went on about the Red, White, and Blue and what it stands for. I didn't really give a shit.

ΔΔΔ

Now, it ain't like I don't like this country, Midge. I love it. But have you seen it lately? Poverty? The crime? The hate? It ain't a new concept. It's just more visible with the Internets and whatnot.

ΔΔΔ

It all went by so fast. I signed up. I blew through Boot Camp. Before I knew it, we were heading to Iran. I ain't never heard much about this place other than the fact that it's some shit hole desert in the middle of nowhere. My unit was decent. They were ready to kill 'hadji' and whatnot. Still not my forte. I'm here to make some money. The paychecks were decent enough to keep the lights on, in a matter of speaking.

One of the things I learned, not to jump ahead, is you don't do this gig for the money. I made more money stocking shelves and pumping gas than I ever did in the Army. I don't even know why I jumped on board. While I suffered through grueling hours of crawling through the mud after waking up before the sun was out, I thought about it. After I was sent out of boot camp and moved on to the next steps of my military life, I still had no idea what the hell I was actually doing this for.

The day came. We were shipping out. I was just excited to be doing something exciting for once, you know? Sitting around with my thumb in my ass wasn't exactly my idea of military life. Sure, we fired guns at targets. Something deep down wanted more of the action. I didn't feel this desire to serve my country. I didn't want to do it for my fellow man. Truth be told, maybe it was some primal need of mine to be in the middle of whatever was going on overseas.

The flight was long. I remember stretching my legs once we landed and thanked whoever was listening that I didn't have to sit in the shithole of a plane any longer. I noticed first how hot it was. Then I noticed the smell. Now, I grew up in some shitty parts of town, but this place took the cake. I'd never smelled anything like this place before. I was pretty sure they were taking a big shit in the middle of the street and walking away from it. It pissed me off, to be honest. I bet this place used to be beautiful.

We set up in some sort of a palace. Some rich dude used to live here back in the day, but we appropriated it for ourselves. Some of the guys were joking about finding the bodies of the kids somewhere in the house and doing something called "skull fucking" them. That's pretty sick if you ask me. What kind of a fucked-up individual would do something like that? To a kids' corpse? Thank god I'm not a sick bastard like these guys.

Two or three of the privates I deployed with actually went through with some nasty shit with the bodies of the dead. I watched it all. They joked, giggled, and had a grand old time. Thank god this wasn't the modern age because this garbage would have been all over the Snapgram or whatever the hell the kids use to share pictures of nasty shit to each other. After they finished up their grabass game, we unloaded and took over rooms of the palace.

The next morning, after a rough night of sleep, we headed out on patrol. I kept thinking about Private Snuffy, Jodi, and Buddy. You may know them as the three dick wads who decided to fuck some kids' dead bodies as a joke. Clothes on or not, that's still fucked up. They were riding in the Humvee with me. They even thought that joking about yesterday's ordeal would be a great idea. All that did was piss me off.

I took time away from listening to them gloat and brag about their victory yesterday and decided to watch out the window. The buildings were all brown. They had rugs hung up at places, but nothing really stuck out. Markets adorned some of the cross streets, where the most traffic was held. I didn't see any people fucking goats or any of the stories they shared with us back home. It was enough to say I was disappointed to see absolutely nothing going on.

I looked down each road. I could see some charming temples or something in the distance, almost glowing green underneath the bright blue sky. Hardly any clouds mottled up the skyline at all. It was almost, dare I say, relaxing? I was actually in a good comfort place. Snuffy and crew wouldn't shut up about everything, and it snapped me back to reality. Buddy was in the gunner seat, scanning around for anything that could kill us.

Apparently, he wasn't doing a good job, because as I looked through the driver's side window across from me, I saw the tail end of the smoke trail of a rocket headed our way. One of the bad guys shot a missile directly at our car. Wasn't nothing we could do but brace for impact. The RPG slammed into the ground just in front of the Humvee. The whole thing flipped right over, and we ended up on our side. Buddy was thrown from the gunner seat and landed somewhere in the street. Bullets cracked out overhead.

My ears were ringing, and I was trying to figure myself out. I was calm. Too calm compared to what the rest of the crew was doing. Most of them spent the next few moments freaking out about the explosion and getting out of their seatbelts. I calmly disengaged my belt and dropped to the door. I crawled out of the gunner hatch and landed hard in the sandy dirt road below. I could hear them struggling to get out of the seats. We didn't have hard armor on the thing like they do now, so we were sitting ducks.

I laid low and headed to some building corner. They had huge stone pillars that supported a balcony just above where I was sitting. I checked myself for any injuries. Free and clear. I managed to escape with all my arms and legs. I could hear more bullets ring out overhead. A few struck the pillar I hid behind. I decided to follow my training and return fire. I felt around for my rifle. *Shit. I left it inside the goddamn seat!* How could I be so stupid? I left the only thing that could get in between me and these towelhead fucks.

I felt around my leg holster. My knife was there waiting for me. I liked this knife, personally. A nice leather grip and a sharp, curved blade. I don't know if I was allowed to have this thing or not, but who the hell was going to tell me no right now? I grabbed the handle, and held the blade facing outward, against my forearm. I've used a knife before. This isn't my first dance. I held my position and hunkered down for a while.

It felt like hours went by sitting behind the pillar. In reality, it was only about a minute or two, but it felt like an eternity. I held my position. I glanced around for Buddy, but he was nowhere to be found. I guess he got ejected pretty far. I heard some commotion from behind the pillar on the opposite side. This was it: go time.

I stood up slowly, clenching my favorite knife in my hands. I closed my eyes for a brief moment and held my breath. Once I opened my eyes, I lunged around the corner, plunging my knife into the first asshole to make the mistake of standing there. The knife slid in, smooth and quick. I opened my eyes and looked my would-be assailant in the eyes.

The eyes looking back at me were a deep green. Snuffy had managed to get out of one of the doors and made his way my direction. Stupid son of a bitch didn't even announce if he was friendly. I just stared at him, with his eyes fixed on mine as he gasped for air like a fish out of water. I slowly removed my blade from his neck and let him sink to the ground. He uselessly grasped at his neck to stop the bleeding, but I aimed to kill. Snuffy wasn't coming back from this one. More bullets struck the top of the pillar that I was now standing in front of. I wiped the knife off on the vest that Snuffy wore. He wasn't going to be worried about the stains.

Another round of bullets hit nearby. They were dialing in the attack. I decided to take shelter behind the Humvee. I crept slowly around the rear side of the vehicle when I was grabbed by the vest by someone. Instinctively, I flailed my knife across whoever had ahold of me. With one vicious slice, I cut into Jodi's face. I cut him from chin to eyebrow, and deep too. He flailed backward from me.

"What the fuck, man?" he screamed as he clenched for his face.

Apparently, I wasn't the only one to hear him scream or see him stagger into the street. One lucky bullet struck Jodi's skull as he clenched his face. His body dropped quickly, and I knew his life was snuffed out right away. I still hadn't seen where Buddy went off to. I wiped my knife back off once more on Snuffy's vest, taking shelter back behind the pillar that I'd hid behind for a while. Bullets continued to whiz through the atmosphere. I figured I was a done deal.

The bullets stopped. The indiscriminate firing rounds blindly into every surface ceased all at once. The silence was almost deafening. It practically caused me pain it was so quiet. I felt around on my body. I wasn't hit, and I wasn't bleeding. It was tough to tell what blood was mine or someone else's at this point. I figured since I felt no pain, that I wasn't hurt. That was the other guy's blood. Snuffy and Jodi's blood. Everything is going to be ok.

I slid out from behind the barricade that I had fortified behind for the past hour or so. Hell, it could have been five minutes for all I knew, but it sure as heck felt like an hour. I looked around. Nothing but silence amidst the blowing dust that had crept in. I heard about these dust storms but never seen one in real life. It was like a fog that you could chew on. I kept my head low and made a dash for the hummer. No bullets or voices could be heard. Maybe they got up and went home?

The vehicle was kicked up on its side. Whatever they used was pretty good to bump this big hunk of shit over. I assumed it was a land mine or some crazy explosive the army gives out. The underside was torn up to shit. I'm no car guy, but I know when something looks out of place. I crept around the backside of the wreck. There was nothing to be found of use, save for some spilled or leaking gasoline. That could have been some other kind of fluid. Who knows? I knelt down low, making my way around the bend, wondering what, or who, was waiting for me on the other side.

I slowly rounded the second corner, revealing the top of this giant metal hunk of shit. The gunners' seat lay parallel to the ground. Halfway pinned under it, I found Private Buddy. I didn't see where he went when we got hit. He was already a done deal, apparently. I probably should have pulled him back inside or something, but it is what it is. This whole thing ain't his problem no more. I heard some rocks crunching off to my right. It had to be the guys responsible for all of this carnage.

I grabbed Buddy's rifle. I figured it would be the smart thing to do since I was armed with my good looks and charming personality. My chiseled jawline wasn't saving us from this one. I checked the rifle, making sure it had ammo. His M-16 was ready to rock and roll. I slung it and crept around the gunner's hatch. My head was on a swivel. I knew these assholes could literally be just about anywhere. As I reached the front of the vehicle, I saw him.

Standing no more than a few feet from my direction, Haji number one was peering through the tire well to see if he could find my body. I'm sure he was looking at the other two, taking a mental note and performing math in his head. I figure he already saw this one hanging out of the top of the hummer. He wasn't paying no mind to me. I decided to do what I figured was my American duty and gave him some red-hot freedom.

I raised the rifle, careful not to let the stupid plastic and metal parts clang around and rattle. I raised the iron sights to put the base of his neck in line with the three pins. I breathed slowly and gently squeezed the trigger. I did everything they trained us to do. After a second of pulling the trigger, I felt the rifle kick back into my shoulder, and let out an audible 'kapow' in my right ear. Instantly, as if being a bag of rocks dropped from a rooftop, he crumpled in front of me. That was interesting. It was the first time I've ever killed anybody. I got my first certified kill.

ΔΔΔ

I see the look you're giving me, Marjory. 'How could I get my first kill when I already done killed all these other people between then and now?' Let me clarify that it was my first sanctioned, government-issued kill. I did it for my country and for my people. So, stop giving me that look and overthinking what I'm telling you. I got more to tell you about this one.

ΔΔΔ

Anywhos, after popping the first guy like a grape, I felt something grip my throat. My heart raced. My blood ran cold. I had no idea what the hell was going on behind me! Instinctively, I threw my left elbow backward, striking the thigh of some unknown assailant. He didn't let his grip slip at all. I struggled for a few moments before feeling mildly faint. I flailed at his hands and arms around my neck. I could see faintly that he was wearing some sort of military gear but couldn't tell what color and who's side he was playing for.

As my eyes began seeing little stars, I had a flash of a thought. My knife! I forgot I put it back in my leg holster. I reached down and felt the hard, rubberized handle. I had never been more relieved to feel that knife than I did at this point. I withdrew the blade from my leg and swung wildly behind me, hoping to stick whatever had a hold on me. I felt a bit of resistance with the second swipe. I decided to rock backward into whoever was around my neck. I'd be giving them more leverage, but they'd also get my full weight pressing into this blade.

As I rocked backward on my heels, I felt the blade sink in deeper. I hit something good. I felt the familiar sticky, warm liquid run over my hands. Blood was pouring from somewhere. I felt the grip on my throat tighten a bit more. I began to feel hazy and faint. I pushed my entire body backward, causing the unknown guy to topple over. If I was going, so was he by god. As the two of us toppled back onto the dirt road, I felt the blade stop sharply against something. I wasn't sure if it was the ground, a rock, or his spine. I didn't have time to figure that out, either. My assailant had closed his grip entirely around my throat, causing my airway to become restricted, and I guess my blood flow to stop going to my brain. I became delusional for a hot second before blacking out all at once.

ΔΔΔ

62

Midge, let me tell you. Combat and the military, that's a whole new monster. I seen some shit out there that made me appreciate how good we have it here in America. If you got kids, I hope they never join the service. Tell em to get good at something here. That's the best advice I can give you, Margaret.

ΔΔΔ

I was blacked out for a while. I assumed I was dead. I mean, I don't know how I thought I was dead or alive. Death is a funny construct because none of us know what it feels like to actually die. We know people have their hearts stop for a moment but can be resuscitated. They talk about an out of body experience, seeing the bright light and shit. But no one knows what it is like to permanently die, only to come back long after. It was sunset. The light blue sky had turned to a blood orange in the fading light of the day. I didn't see any bright lights, no pearly gates. Just darkness. I can only assume I didn't die.

I moved my head a bit. The guy I remember resting upon before my last moments on this Earth was gone. Hell, I wasn't even in the same place I fell over at. I was on one of them hospital gurney boards. It seems our convoy didn't come back, and lost track of our vehicle. They sent a rescue party out for us. Well, they sure as shit didn't sign up for all of this. I looked around as the guys tried to clean up and retrieve what they could. Every time I moved my head, I could feel how sore my throat was.

As I laid out next to one of the hospital hummers, some guy came up to me. He sat on the edge of the bumper and started asking me questions. I had a massive ringing in my head and wasn't in the mood to say much.

"Hey Private, you're going to be ok," I remember him saying. "It's a real miracle you survived all of this. The savages can be known to do some downright disgusting things. We are going to get you back to base and get you home, roger?"

I held my hand up and gave my best attempt as a thumbs up. Did they really assume this was all just those two guys? Am I a goddamn war hero? Christ, I was not cut out for that kind of title. It wasn't like I had much choice, and the vehicle closed up and rode away.

ΔΔΔ

So, all in all, Peg, I told them it was all Snuffy who went down in a blaze of glory. Sure, I had the one guy choke me out, and Snuffy threw me a knife to save myself, but it was he who was the real hero. One hell of a soldier. He was awarded some posthumous shit, and I got to sit in the hospital for a few weeks somewhere in Italy before going home. I was discharged but instructed to go to therapy and talk to people about it. I figured I was good enough to leave the hospital, I'm good enough to face the world. I had a life to live. I saw enough while I was in to understand that I could use the military card to get into school and get a better life. I was going to do just that. I needed to be a better person than my non-existent father or shitty chain-smoking mother was. They must have lost me in the shuffle because I was never contacted about going to rehab or therapy since. I discovered how good the Army was about missing documents and records.

Matter of fact, I looked me up a few weeks ago. I can't find a goddamn thing on me. Nothing about the incident, the medals, or my injuries. I'm like a goddamn ghost. Good job, records department. Good job.

Chapter 6

Entry 106

After I drifted a while off and on, I finally settled down in a nice little spot in the Midwest. I decided I wanted to spend my days dodging tornados and rednecks. I'm not sure what caused me to come to this decision, but I just felt like it was a good step. After the falling out I had with the military and the job at the florist shop, I about had it with Florida and everything it had to offer. I spent at least three of the best years of my life wasting away doing useless tasks to try to make my life better. What the hell did I have to show for it? Christ, Marge. The least you could do is offer some sort of condolence or supporting 'there, there.' Nothing. Much like everyone I knew in life.

ΔΔΔ

I moved into a really nice apartment building. I say it was really nice because it had air conditioning and free cable included with my rent. I never had those comforts growing up. I was really branching out into the modern man's world! I had a decent amount of cash on me from the odd jobs I took up before moving. I was able to save some money by hitchhiking across the states. They always warn you to be careful with hitching. You never know what kind of crazy person will pick you up. They might not take you to your destination. Luckily, I ended up just fine, and settled into a new life.

I went to the local Woolworth for some household goods. I needed cleaners, blankets, towels, and utensils. I had no idea how much stuff ordinary people had in their day to day lives until I walked into a bare-bones empty apartment. I didn't have a bed, tables, or any furniture to speak of. Those things would come later, but for now, it was best to just grab some of the basics.

The Woolworth was tucked away in a small shopping center, surrounded by a bunch of other local stores. There was a local drug store, a barber, and some diner squeezed in on the corner. I made a mental note to eat there one day when I wasn't schlepping grocery bags of shit back home. I was taking in my surroundings and not paying attention. I ran square into the door, which was two-thirds of the way ajar.

"I am so sorry!" a voice shouted from inside.

I was still recovering from trying to go through a solid object. I didn't even see the young lady on the other end of the door, still holding it open.

"I walked into it myself. Not your fault at all," I responded as I nursed my face and shoulder.

I did my best to laugh it off, but it hurt like a sonofabitch. She could tell I wasn't letting on enough that it really hurt. I wasn't no pussy. I could take the pain. I've been to war and hit by some large sedan, after all. Thankfully, people in Florida don't like dealing with insurance much, and would instead settle things with cash. I told him my head and legs were hurting until I saw enough bills in my hand to feel better. He drove away in the brown Cadillac, and I walked away a few thousand dollars richer. His fault, though.

His blonde secretary was blowing him while he drove. I guess he didn't want his wife to find out. *Dirtbag.*

"Let me take you inside and grab you some ice from behind the counter," she said as she took my hand and led me inside.

Before I knew it, I was waiting near the cash registers, holding a cold compress against my head. I didn't need it, but I enjoyed the hospitality. To say humanity and other gestures that regular people do would be lost on me is an absolute lie. I appreciate people being friendly to me, and I enjoy doing the same. I've always loved working with customers. I just enjoy working with a small frequency of them. That's why I felt right at home with night shifts at the five and dime. I'd still get people, but I also had long spurts of being left alone.

I decided I had enough of being taken care of and left my bag of ice on the countertop. I started for the shopping carts when I was grabbed on the wrist from behind.

"Feeling better?" the young girl asked.

She had to be at least a few years younger than I was. Here I was, pushing thirty, and she had to be in her early twenties. She had long red hair and the greenest eyes I'd ever seen. I wasn't sure how to really talk to women. It was so easy with Blondie since me and her had that little icebreaker of me saving her life.

"I guess. I just need to buy towels."

Towels? I need to buy towels? What the fuck am I? Towels. Who the hell says that? I just released an awkward smile from my mouth and shuffled over to the shopping carts. I said I was good with people, but I didn't mention how high my skill level was. Ginger waved to me with a smile and went back to work sweeping out the front door. I kept my head down and went on with my duties to stock my apartment.

I rolled my cart down the aisle for home goods. I grabbed some sponges and dish soap. Probably a good call for when I decide to get some dishes. I grabbed linens. I picked up bed sheets, curtains, and a few rugs. I also grabbed the bath and kitchen towels. In my travels down the aisles, I found a quality set of dishes and pots and pans. I was proud of myself. This was the first time I've ever actually shopped for my own belongings. Mother was usually the one to do all of this when she did. It was liberating, in a way.

I rounded out my shopping list grabbing soaps and other necessities for the bathroom. It occurred to me I lacked a toothbrush and toothpaste for that matter. I wheeled my loot up to the front counter. The shopping cart towered and swayed as I made each turn. A careful balance was made to not topple as I stopped in front of the front counter. Ginger was there to greet me.

"Woah, a lot of stuff to pick up, I see!"

I smiled. "Yeah, it is. Just moving into a new place," I bashfully responded.

She popped her chewing gum, nodding her head in approval.

"Right on."

She began to load my things into bags as she rang up each item. By the time we were done, I had about fifteen bags full of shit I probably didn't even need. She pressed the total button on the register.

"Tell ya what. I'll hook you up with my discount," Ginger smiled and said as she mashed on the keys a bit.

I watched the total price drop by a decent chunk. I paid for everything with the cash I had on me and awaited the receipt.

"Here. And there's a little something on the back for you too," she said, sliding me the receipt.

I flipped it over, and her number was on the back. I don't know how but in some way, I was a lady killer. Slaying all of them without even trying. I sure as heck lacked the social skills to do what I did, but if looks could kill, apparently I'd be a murderer.

"Thanks," I awkwardly let out, smiling as I tried to bundle all of the bag handles onto my forearm to carry.

"Are you parked close? I could have someone give you a hand," Ginger said as she began to greet the next person.

"No, I'm fine. I only live a few blocks from here. It's not a far walk."

"Walk? Oh no, my man. Gag me with a spoon. You don't have a car?"

I looked down at my feet for a moment. I barely had time to get better clothes than the ones I purchased in a hurry as I headed away from Florida. It's not like I had a washing machine or the means to clean clothes. Purchasing new ones seemed reasonable at that time.

"No. I walked from my apartment. I just moved in, actually," I humbly said, trying to adjust some of the bags on my arm.

She paused, ringing up the next customer. I saw her actively thinking for a moment.

"My shift ends in thirty minutes. I could give you a lift, and maybe get some dinner? I assume you don't have food in your brand-new place?" Ginger asked, eying the bags of necessities I just procured.

"Correct."

"Killer. Let's do it. I'll put your bags back here, and we can get out of this place at four."

Ginger grabbed for my bags and she placed them behind the counter and out of the way, two by two. I heard her apologize to the older lady that was behind me as I wandered off to the lawn and garden section. I figured it was a good idea to just relax and pass the time in a folding lawn lounger.

ΔΔΔ

I tell ya, Margaret. That place had everything. Few places I miss more than I miss Woolworth's. I miss Montgomery Wards too. That's where I eventually got some of my furniture and appliances. It was dying off though, you could see the signs. Almost like how Sears looks today, know what I mean?

ΔΔΔ

Ginger greeted me, now without her teal collared work shirt. She was officially free to leave. I followed her back up to the front of the store and gathered as many bags as I could. She grabbed a few handfuls herself. I did my best to prevent her from carrying too many bags. She motioned her head to follow her outside to the parking lot.

"It's the little blue one over there," she said as we stepped off the curb.

Ahead of us in the parking lot sat a beautiful, deep blue 1973 Chevelle coup, complete with a cream-colored interior. It was a beautiful car. I never fancied myself a car guy until this very moment. I've never wanted to fuck a car before, but by God, this car could get it. I know it would never work, being I don't have the parts and all, and well, the car doesn't either. But that's how beautiful this thing was. Ginger really had good taste in automobiles.

"Beautiful car you got here. Mind if I see under the hood?" I ask excitedly.

She popped the trunk with her keys and tossed them to me.

"Sure, knock yourself out."

I fumbled the keys into the driver's side lock and opened it. The door creaked open with the howl of a proper American made machine. The interior was clean. The car was cared for. I carefully reached inside and popped the hood. I slowly walked over to the hood, released the level, and pulled open the heavy metal hood. I engaged the prop rod and stared back at the pristine, clean engine compartment.

"Christ. Look at that. Your boyfriend really knows how to take care of a car!" I said stupidly.

She closed the trunk after loading the last of the groceries, meeting me at the driver's door.

"My boyfriend is an idiot, which is why I don't have one. This is all me, buddy," she said coyly, resting on the top of the door.

I shrugged and twisted my mouth in an expression of shock and approval. I gently closed down the hood and walked toward the passenger door. Honestly, I know car guys that don't have a car that clean under the hood. Especially kids these days, they don't know how to clean chrome if it bit them in the ass.

"Where to?" Ginger asked as I sat in the car.

I shrugged. I couldn't recommend anywhere aside from the diner on the corner of this cozy strip mall we were at. I don't know if it was the polite thing to do, or if she just forgot that I was extremely new here.

"No ideas? That's fine, let's try the mall," Ginger said to me as she turned the engine.

The engine fired up with a thunderous roar. It was enough to piss off neighbors if they were asleep. I'm sure her neighbors were pissed, actually. She clearly works early shifts. I didn't care, nor did I mind. This thing was rumbling with a massive set of balls hanging on the back of it. I felt the power as she smashed the gas pedal to the ground. Ginger here was a speed demon.

We got to the mall in record time. I can only assume it was record time because we blew through two stoplights, ran a red light, and musta been doing an easy 80mph the whole damn way. I even may have shit a little. I've been to war. I've seen shit, but I ain't seen no shit like that driving. She was a wild woman behind the wheel. I would say I was terrified, but I was also equally turned on by the whole thing too. She managed this several ton death machine with finesse.

ΔΔΔ

Did I mention that I loved that car? I would have almost done anything for that car, Margie. It was a masterpiece of American craftsmanship. I actually grabbed a few of them Chevelle models here and there, but none were ever in such a condition as Ginger's ride was.

ΔΔΔ

The mall was huge. We pulled up to this massive mega-structure with a huge parking lot. There was so much building, I never saw anything like it before. Sure, we had shopping malls back home and in Florida, but I never really paid any mind to go in them. This was a monument to the consumer industrial complex that we've created. Outside, it was lined with beautiful trees and topiaries. The parking lot was paved nicely, with neon lights running the lengths of the building at points. It was like something out of a movie.

Ginger parked the car, and we quickly made our way to the entrance. The automatic doors slid apart, revealing what I thought was heaven. I must have died at some point. This was a great place! A fifteen-foot-high water fountain greeted us beyond the vestibule. Old people and children huddled around it, throwing pennies in for useless wishes that would never come true.

I felt Ginger grip my left hand and pull me along. She was eager to show me something in this mall, and who was I to stop her? There was a crazy variety of characters that lined the mall. I saw the rock and roll, the preppy, and the stoner loser type. They had the nerdy, the old, the young, and the in-between. This was the Mecca of the area. Everyone flocked to this spot.

As I people watched, we pushed past the entrance of a Radio Shack, Payless Shoes, and some bright clothing stores. She pulled me through the food court, passing the Orange Julius, A&W Rootbeer, and a Taco Bell. If we weren't here to shop or eat, what the hell were we doing here?

"Ok, hang on," I said, pulling my hand away to stop.

"Is something wrong? I need to check something out before we eat," Ginger replied.

I guess the puzzled look on my face said it all.

"A new album came out, and I really want it. I've been waiting for this one!"

Music had never been my thing, save for my Ratt album I was gifted. I never put much stock in listening to anything on the radio. Silence was good enough for me. I usually heard music playing in public places, but I couldn't tell you who was singing or the title of the track.

"Ok, well, let's get moving then," I said as I pushed forward past her in the direction we were headed.

Ginger stopped in front of this store called Sam Goody. I don't know who Sam was, or what was so good about him, but I guess he sold a lot of music. We crossed the threshold and was immediately greeted by music playing over some speakers. It was some hip-hop song that came out, I guess.

"Go find something you like! I have to get my hands on this before it's gone," Ginger said excitedly as she squatted down with her hands in front of her, a smile ear to ear.

She ran off toward some aisle and began flipping through the records. I didn't even know where to begin, so I just started at the furthermost aisle. I shuffled through Blues, Country, and Classical. A few names sounded familiar, at least from school. I knew Beethoven, Bach, and other classics. I'd heard of B.B. King. I poked through a few and flipped through a handful of albums before moving on to the next aisle.

Rock and Roll was the title of the next section. I knew a bit about this, so I felt comfortable looking through for something. I saw a few things from the likes of Ozzy Osbourne, Kiss, and Bon Jovi. One album caught my eye, however. It was two half faces, in black and white. Some guys named Hall and Oates. I thought that was a unique choice of name, personally. Someone was in love with architecture and grains that much? Not until I read the back of the album cover did I realize that was the names of the two guys whose faces were halved on the front of the cover.

"You want to give it a listen? That's a great album, my man!" the kid from the store said to me.

He had long blonde hair and grungy looking leather on. A star-shaped earring dangled from one ear. I bet the ladies loved this shit. Here I was wearing jeans and a dusty grey t-shirt.

"Oh, yeah. The Halls and Oat guys are awesome. Is this album any good?" I stupidly asked.

"Hall and Oates. And yes, sir. Private Eyes is a great album. Came out a while ago, but I chill out to them when I want to bring a lady over if you know what I mean."

I rubbed my chin and nodded my head as I looked back at the album. I had no idea what type of music this really was. I was over my head and out of my element.

"Is there anything else you recommend? I'm into just about anything that sounds good," I safely responded.

His face lit up. Either he took me as a fool that he could push a stack of music onto, or he was delighted that his opinion was valued. I didn't really give a shit either way, I just wanted to kill time while I waited for Ginger. I spotted her with giant headphones on her ears, enjoying some new song. I assume she found what she was looking for. She gave me a thumbs up with a giant smile. Some people have a happy place, and this must have been hers.

Good Hair Goody employee led me over to a few other things. Without question, he began to stack up a few records in my arms. I couldn't tell him I didn't like it, because frankly, I didn't even know what the hell he stuck in my arms. We wandered through three more aisles, and he put at least five albums in my hands. Thank god I had a wallet full of cash, or I'd be upset about him milking me for what I had. I didn't look like I was made of money, so I assumed he genuinely wanted to help.

After a few more laps around the store, he led me to the register. Ginger was slowly walking over to join me after listening to the entire album, I assume. She had one record and a cassette tape in her hands. Once she joined back up with me, I could tell she was eyeing up my new collection.

"Ooh, a regular connoisseur, I see. Whatcha got?" she said as she curiously thumbed through the collection.

"I dunno. He just started throwing stuff my way."

Ginger flipped through the stack and had to remark on every single one.

"Ooh, look at you! Stryper, Hall and Oates, Beastie Boys? You're just all over the place, aren't you?" she jested, "Thriller? That's a solid get. Michael Jackson is one of the greats. Wham! I love Wham!"

I smiled. This guy knew how to put together an excellent selection, apparently. It appears Ginger approved of the collection I was soon to leave with. Goody Guy finished ringing up each of my albums, placing them into a slick black bag, with a giant red logo of the store name emblazoned on the side.

"Oh, this one too!" I said, grabbing Ginger's album.

She looked utterly shocked as I pulled her purchase in with my own and footed the bill for the whole lot of it.

"You didn't have to do that, you know," she scolded.

I shrugged. I knew I didn't, but I figured it was a decent gesture I could do. She did give me a lift after all.

Goody Guy flipped his long blonde hair back behind his ear and shoulder, waiting for the next instructions. I waved him on to continue adding her item to my transaction. It was the least I could do.

He placed her album in a separate bag and handed me my own. I grabbed Ginger's bag and turned to give it to her, only to be met with a scowl.

"You don't have to take care of me. I can afford it myself, dude," she fumed.

I still didn't know why she was so upset. I began to slowly walk out of the store, unsure of what I did wrong. She wanted something, I got it for her. As I crossed the entryway of the store and entered the mall once more, she grabbed me by the forearm.

"Hey, sorry about that. I'm just not used to that," she said apologetically.

I smiled to ease her mind. The fact she apologized made me feel a bit better too.

"I figure since you drove me all the way over here that I should return the favor where I could."

"Fair enough, dude. Fair enough."

Once the tension was cut through, the mood between the two of us began to improve. We sauntered toward the food court. It really felt that the feeling was unanimous that we were hungry and should take care of that issue as quickly as possible.

We passed by several clothing stores and armies of teenagers that lingered around just about everywhere. Soft music played in the background, but I couldn't make out exactly what it was.

"What are you in the mood for?" Ginger asked.

I realized we were approaching the food court. I started scanning around at the restaurant names, trying to decipher what they sold. Some of it was straight forward. I assumed Taco Bell served some sort of tacos. The Burger King sold hamburgers. A&W sounded like the root beer company, which, as it turns out, was the root beer company.

"Let's get some Chinese?" Ginger asked, pointing to the place with the foreign writing and a giant panda as a logo.

I've never eaten anything outside of hamburgers, chicken nuggets, and things I fully understood. Hot dogs were even dicey for me because I didn't know what they crammed into them, but I still enjoyed them. I guess it was the 'American Way' to enjoy them. I considered expanding my pallet.

"I'm not sure I've ever had that stuff. Isn't that made of cat?" I asked, as serious as I could.

Ginger wasn't sure how to respond. I think my question either made her uncomfortable or made her think about something that never once crossed her mind. I decided to let out a small smile.

"Jerk. You're going to ruin that food for me forever, you know that?"

"I couldn't help it. In all seriousness, I never ate that before. What else is here?" I asked, changing the subject.

Ginger looked around. Her eyes stopped on each respective restaurant, perusing their menu before walking over.

"No. I made up my mind. Chinese. Cat or not," Ginger said, as she started confidently toward the China Hut.

I hesitantly followed. There were so many smells that wafted through the air, it was intoxicating and sickening at the same time. She stopped at the rear of the line, behind some guy wearing an excessive amount of jewelry.

"Get the Sweet and Sour Chicken. Trust me," she said, glancing back to me.

Trust her? I barely knew this girl. We go all the way back to at least three hours ago. I'd never had much success in dating women. I didn't even know how I landed these girls. Blondie was at the right time and place. So was Ginger, apparently. I didn't realize it at the time, but this ended up being the trend of my life. People just gravitated toward me. They wanted to hear what I had to say. They wanted to know more.

We ordered and sat at some booth in the food court. My Coke was pretty good, at least. I can't say the same for the food. I poked and picked at the chicken, ultimately eating the rice from around it. Ginger didn't say anything. I sure as hell wasn't going to bring it up either. It was my money, my waste.

"You want to get out of here?" Ginger casually asked.

I finished the rest of my Coke and gave a confirming head nod. We picked up our purchases and moved out of the food court, pitching our trash in the can on the way out.

"I need to get a new pair of work pants, do you mind?" Ginger asked as she pointed to a clothing store just around the bend.

Now that she said something, I needed clothes too. I owned two pairs of clothes to my name. The ones on my back, and the others I had to throw away when I arrived. They were covered in dirt, mud, and blood. Couldn't very well be cruising the shopping mall in those threads, could I?

"I need some things too. Let's do it," I said as I gripped my albums in my hand. The bag was already getting sticky and gross from my sweat.

She didn't really put up a fight in changing the type of store she was going to go to. We ended up looking at some big store, named J.C. Penny. There was something here for everyone. Ginger wandered off toward the ladies' department. I started shuffling through the menswear. I never really had to buy my own clothes. At my age, I should have gone through at least two wardrobe changes by now. Leaving your whole life behind and starting over really puts a damper on that. That, and military time. They gave me everything I needed.

I looked at just about everything. Suits. I'm not a suit guy. At least, I wasn't sure I was a suit guy. I circled back to the formal wear. I had no idea what the hell I was doing. I usually wore some slacks, jeans, or a plain polo shirt. I never wore anything proper, ya know.

ΔΔΔ

Now that I think about it, Midge, I did wear formal clothes a few times. I wore a set of nice clothes to a funeral for a neighbor my ma was friends with. After this adventure at Penny's, I started to have an affinity for looking nice from time to time. I broke up my Adidas branded clothing with the occasional pinstripe suit. I wanted to look dapper, and goddamnit I did. I was a sexy motherfucker, Margery.

ΔΔΔ

One of the attendants came to my aid. He luckily guided me into stylish clothing design and even got me a shopping cart. I left with two pristine suits, some undershirts, dress shirts, and some t-shirts. I also grabbed a few pairs of jeans while I was there. Can't look dapper all the time. Sometimes you need to dress down. I figured I should head to the other side of the store and link back up with Ginger.

I tracked her down, looking at some scarves and mittens. We were months away from winter, but hey, better to be safe than sorry, I guess.

"Nice hat!" I said jokingly about the giant winter headpiece she donned. It was bulky, complete with a giant poof ball on the top.

Ginger quickly snatched it away from her head.

"I was just checking things out. I need a new hat for winter. I can wait on that," she said, gripping the pairs of pants she held in one arm tighter, "I got what I need."

She glanced around at the abundance of things I was towing around in a cart. I had everything from suits to jeans. I had a pair of P.F. Flyers to wear on my feet. I was actually going to have a closet full of clothing.

"You really are just starting over, aren't you?"

"Yeah. I left my old life behind after I joined the Army."

She wrinkled her brow a bit. "A soldier, huh? I never took you for the type."

"Yeah, went to Iraq. Nothing exciting. Now I'm here."

We started to walk toward the cashier area with our purchases as we made small talk.

"So, what's it like?" Ginger asked.

"What like?"

"Iraq. Anywhere but here. Is it different?"

I paused. I wasn't sure how to answer this question. I'd been just about everywhere in between moving here and leaving Florida. I drifted for quite a while before settling down here.

"Uh, well, it's different," I safely answered, knowing damn well she was going to want more.

"Different!" she laughed, "That doesn't answer the question, dude. Is it more exciting? Is it dangerous? I've always wanted to know what it's like to live in a big city."

I've lived in big cities. I've lived in small towns. I even lived in the middle of friggin nowhere. It's all the same. As long as you're in that place, you'll transform your brain to enjoy it. The problem is when you don't know any better, and you're stranded in the same shit town for the rest of your life. This girl needs to see the world.

"You should visit New York or something. It's intense!" I lied. I never been to New York. At least, not at the time.

"New York! That would be too fancy for me," Ginger said as she placed her belongings on the counter for the cashier, "what, with Broadway and Times Square. I just wouldn't fit in."

I handed the cashier cash for my purchase. I didn't offer to pay for Ginger's items this time.

"I'm sure you'd love it up there. There's so much going on, and you seem like you'd be into that sort of thing."

Ginger shrugged. She gathered her bag from the cashier, thanked them, and headed for the door slowly. She allowed me time to catch up with all of my bags.

"Let's get you home before you spend all of your money!"

I laughed. Ginger was right. I probably blew through a few hundred today alone. It was perhaps best. We made our way through the crowds of misfits, delinquents, and the elderly. We pushed our way through the giant glass doors that led outside. The sun had begun to set already and was low in the sky.

"Wow, look at that," Ginger said, staring off at the sinking sunset.

I never really took in a sunset myself. The way the orange bleeds into the sky, coating even the clouds in a maroon shade. Couple that with the shadows created on the skyline by the sunset, it makes for a breathtaking sight. I barely realized she started making her way to the car. I watched as she fiddled with the keyring to find the trunk key. She popped it open after a few jingles and tries.

On the way home, we listened to the radio. She turned it up on a particular song. I assumed it was something she liked. The song was catchy sounding, with some synthetic instruments playing. Some guy, or guys singing. It wasn't bad.

"This is your jam, isn't it?" Ginger asked.

My face must have given everything away. Ginger looked over from her seat into my eyes.

"Private Eyes! Hall and Oates? Didn't you totally just buy the album?"

I glanced down at the radio as if looking for a clue. This was who that was? At least it was decent to listen to. My expression changed to a smile, and I began to enjoy the song.

ΔΔΔ

Let me tell you, Marge. That girl, Ginger, she was a real keeper. She liked fast cars, good tunes and dressed nice. And her perfume. Don't even get me started on the aroma. Once she dropped me off, I unloaded about four thousand shopping bags into the apartment and began to put things in place. I still needed furniture, but at least I had clothes and the means to cook and eat food. That was a hell of a start.

I saw Ginger a few times off and on, but nothing serious ever came from it. I'd like to think it was mostly my fault. I've never been good with women. I wasn't with Blondie, and I sure as hell wasn't with Ginger. It's not that she wasn't my type, its that I never knew how to approach the topic. I blame my mother for that one. She never really let me have friends, let alone girlfriends. If you want to go down that rabbit hole, doc, I'm more than happy to explore that one later.

Anywho, I ended up going to this giant store, Montgomery Wards. They had just about everything. I had some of the people from their store deliver some furniture. I grabbed a bed, a dresser, as well as a dining room table. I got this really sweet couch. Name brand, too. It was salmon-colored, long. Wasn't no cheap Ikea or something like the kids are into these days. The damn couch was indestructible. I miss that couch.

Chapter 7

Entry 109

I had to clean up the blood. There was so much of it. Who knew a human could hold so much of it? Standing in the four-bedroom family home, I was at a loss for ideas. Did they have a washing machine? Did they have a shit load of towels? Fucking sororities. They probably had plenty of alcohol and drugs, though. I had to think quickly how to get myself out of this mess. How do I always find myself in the middle of this type of shit?

I remember driving past the place. I purchased some beater car in cash from some guy that was selling it in the paper. It had some seventy thousand miles on it. The rear window didn't roll down, and the passenger side wiper blade was dead. The defrosters didn't work. If you tried to remove the early morning white moisture from the windows, you were greeted by a loud clicking from under the dash. Christ, I hated that car.

The sorority house was always throwing a wild rager every Friday and Saturday night. I don't know how these kids did it. They'd party hard until the early morning light, not waking up until the afternoon. The first ones to stir to life would clean the yard a bit of the beer cans and other assorted garbage, only to get right back to where they were just the night prior. Blew my mind, ya know? Waste of life if you ask me.

I watched some of these girls come and go from the house. Some would leave in brightly colored hot pants, while others left in nothing more than their pajamas. Did they not have any self-worth? Couldn't they dress a little more proper? The lack of effort and the shit they gave about their life reminded me of one thing: Mother. She never dressed nice and was an embarrassment to me anytime we had to go out in public together when I was younger. Thank god she stopped attending my doctor appointments, letting her child ride the public transit alone.

I got the sad feeling these girls didn't care about themselves. Such a damn shame to be, what, eighteen, nineteen years old and given up on life? Why else would you sit home late at night eating junk food? Why spend your days wearing sleepwear? It pissed me off, quite frankly. Here I was, struggling with life, and these girls just wanted to throw it away. Drinking, smoking, fucking; you name it. They did it.

The sorority was located in a friendly, quiet neighborhood about an hour from where I lived. I happened upon it one day by pure accident. I stumbled on this place only because they were in a "post-party" clean up phase. I had been trying to figure out this college thing once again. I needed to get myself right. I wanted to do more with my life. After touring another campus, I found an in. This place really loved taking in former soldiers and was super eager to bring me on. I was in such a good mood that seeing these ladies cleaning their yard as they stumbled around perplexed me.

I had been going to this school for roughly two months. I would hazard a guess I drove by the house at least three to four times a week, at minimum. Sometimes I'd wait until after my classes. Other times I'd creep through between classes. I had the most time after my math course. Frankly, driving cleared my head after that class. Between the course material and the asshole professor, it was more than plenty to increase my blood pressure.

The nineties were a strange time. There was a transition present throughout the whole world. If you didn't keep up on it, you'd completely get lost in the dust. The hair metal, as they called it, was being replaced by some new music now named grunge. I wasn't much of a fan of the new music, but then again, I wasn't much of a fan of music in general. It took me a while to catch up to the world.

These sorority girls didn't have an issue with music. They played the loudest, most obnoxious pop music the world could crank out. Christ, it was like nails on a friggin' chalkboard. Something about the loud noise, mixed with annoying vocal work made me shiver. Almost as irritating as that math professor. His voice could get under my skin too. It was mundane, monotone, and just dull. It's bad enough the topic was tiresome as it were.

As I stood in the doorway of one of the bedrooms, I decided I was a little worn out. I stepped over two of the girls that lay sprawled over each other, coated in red, sticky blood. It was pretty disgusting how they would just ruin a perfectly good rug like that. Down the stairs were two more of the girls, one hanging by her foot over the banister. The other splayed across the landing and two steps. At least they had the decency to not be as messy. I also suppose using the meat tenderizer I found in their kitchen helps with the mess. Knives have always been a disaster to use, as I've learned.

Carefully, I crept over the lifeless body of some brunette that laid on her back in front of the door. She was the one who greeted me. I never wanted to lie about my intentions or falsify credentials. I didn't show up as a delivery man or the pizza guy. I simply got up the nerve on one of the days between parties and knocked on the door. I introduced myself by name. I was polite, friendly, and courteous. I did not act out of character. I'm a nice guy.

Once I broke her nose with the door, thrusting it her direction with my shoulder, I grabbed ahold of her skull. I began to press my thumbs into her eyes. The eyelids provided some sort of resistance, but once my full weight was into it, they gave way. I felt a slipping 'pop' sensation, and she stopped fighting back. I hit something important. Thankfully, I wore a pair of really nice gloves so I didn't get any head goo on my hands.

I was also wearing my most excellent P.F. Flyers, as the kids would say. I didn't want to ruin those, so I picked up some of those booties that I've seen painters wear while restoring some of the buildings in the city. I stole a handful from a box in a science lab at school, figuring they wouldn't miss them. I don't think I planned to do what happened that day, I just like to be prepared and kept 'em in my car for a while.

As I headed through the house, I looked around to locate the kitchen. I was getting a little hungry and wanted to make a sandwich. I turned the light to the kitchen on, and it buzzed loudly. The fridge didn't prove to have anything useful inside. I managed to grab some fancy rye bread and slathered some mayo on it. I topped it with some orange cheese and a slice or two of bologna.

ΔΔΔ

I never understood bologna, Margie. I get ham, turkey, chicken. They all make sense. What the hell was bologna? Matter of fact; don't answer that. I don't think I want to know. I only wish I had better skills in the kitchen. Sandwiches weren't out of my wheelhouse.

ΔΔΔ

I ate my bologna on rye. One hell of a combination, I tell ya. As I took bites, I figured I should take a seat. I cleared the body off the kitchen table. It took some work because I used a friggin' knife before I found that tenderizer. I wedged that knife so deep into this girl's abdomen, it stuck into the table. I barely remembered that one. Don't give me that look. I know what you're thinking. This whole thing is a bit excessive, especially with what I did up at the university earlier. I don't even want to get into the disaster I left up there.

As I finished up my sandwich, I took a good hard look around this house. These chicks really knew how to party, let me tell you that much. I washed my hands and arms of all the blood. There was so much of it pouring into the kitchen sink; it was absurd. I realized that a small amount of Palmolive wasn't going to fix this problem. I shut the faucet off and made my way through the carnage back up the stairs. I rounded the large staircase and proceeded toward the shower. I didn't realize I was that messy. There has to be a better way to keep from getting bloody.

ΔΔΔ

As I showered, I thought about all the girls I killed. A bunch of dumb brunettes. What happened to the ole' 'Busty Blonde' sorority girl? I didn't peg a natural blonde in the mix at all. Is it so much to ask for just a little variety? I mean, shit, Margaret. Here you are, with your boring, dull, and drab brown curls. Par for the course, I assume. At least you don't just have some bullshit bangs. That drives me nuts. Do something with your fucking hair, for Christ's sake.

The sheer fact they didn't care about themselves was the final nail in the coffin. Nobody is gonna miss these girls, save for the jock ass wipes that show up for some pussy. I highly doubted it was going to make the news. Little did I know, it went national. Honestly, looking back, this was the first thing that went national for me. I'll let you in on a little secret though, Midge. I just realized this shit happened a while ago. I must be losing my goddamn mind, can you believe it? I must be going fucking crazy.

I think it was right before the turn of the eighties I did this little number. Hell, this was, remember, when I talked about moving down south? Did I talk about that? Anyway, I did all this shit, and some ass clown took fucking credit for it. Some lawyer cat out of like California or Oregon or some shit. At first, I felt terrible for the kid. He was actually older than me at the time, but I look back and say kid. Turns out, he did some really fucked up stuff out there on the west coast. I didn't even know there were others like me. Talk about eye-opening, Madge.

Chapter 8

Entry 110

I ended up seeing Ginger off and on for the better part of four years. I watched the world change once again. This time we shifted from neon and leather to baggy clothing and flannel. The nineties were a strange time, looking back. The music changed. The kids with their slang evolved. Margie, let me tell you, I hated all the change. I found myself spending too much time trying to keep up with the changes. Luckily, Ginger helped me along with all of that. It blew her mind that I'd never really seen too many movies or listened to music. Hell, I didn't even watch a lot of TV. I found myself out of the loop more often than not.

ΔΔΔ

I took up working at the Woolworth with Ginger. That was a decent job, and I loved what I did. Even though I had a ton of cash, I liked being able to replenish what I was spending with a weekly paycheck. It had been a while since I worked for a steady paycheck, and the feeling I had was one of self-accomplishment. I hadn't had that in a while.

Eventually, I moved out of my apartment and got a place together with Ginger. I more or less owned my old place by paying in cash with so much in advance, so I maintained that in the background. My new endeavor was to move on with my life. I was getting a little older and wanted to settle down, or at least begin to put down some sort of root. I'm not sure what shifted in me, but I wanted to have more order in my life.

We moved into a quaint little townhome that was just on the outskirts of town. It wasn't urbanized by any means, but they definitely knew how to pack them in on this side of town. It was an upgrade from my apartment, I can tell you that much. Having stairs was a game-changer, as well as a back yard. I'd been living on my own, in alleyways, near truck stops, the barracks, and an apartment. This was the first time I had felt a sense of normalcy.

Like I said, I was working alongside Ginger while at the Woolworth. Frankly, I enjoyed myself every day. I performed routine tasks like carrying bags to cars, returning carts, and stocking shelves. Nothing too taxing, ya know? I already told the boss I didn't want to be put on the registers. I don't really want to be near a register, all things considered from my past. Last time I held one in my hands, I put it through someone's thinking piece.

One such day in particular, if I recall, it was in the spring. One of the things I always hated about this season was the amount of rain we'd get. Today was no exception to the rule. It was pouring. On the radio we'd have playing soft music in the stockroom, the guys would bring on a weather report and talk about potential flooding. It was a little wet outside, suffice to say.

The rain wasn't letting up, and even our beautiful little shopping center wasn't immune to its own waterborne troubles. I worked hard to use what I could to mop up the water that poured in from underneath the loading dock door. It was weatherproofed enough, but clearly not designed for a biblical flood.

I mopped. I blotted. Hell, I woulda sandbagged like I did in the Army if I coulda. This shit wasn't stopping. I removed my work polo to get more physical. I began moving some of the damageable paper goods from the floor and placing them on top shelves. I bent down and grabbed packs of Kleenex, paper towels, napkins, and toilet paper and began moving them to the far side of the room, stacking them on a shelf. It was exhausting.

I started to feel overheated and exhausted. The back room wasn't too forgiving in the way of cool breezes and drafts, I can tell you that much. Shit, I woulda killed for a small fan at this point. I felt the sweat rings forming on my white undershirt as I worked. I knew it was in the store's best interests to save all the shit I could. I know it costs money, and I wouldn't want to be replacing the stock. I'm just here doing my civic duty, ya know?

ΔΔΔ

Marge, I got a hell of a work ethic. I might have always liked the night shift at the gas station, but dammit, I worked my ass off. Those shelves were cleaned, floors mopped, and product stocked by the morning. My boss loved me because the store was always ready for the morning rush. The suits that would rush in didn't pay no mind to how clean it was, but I guaran-god-damn-tee you that if it were the other way around, they'd be losing their shit.

ΔΔΔ

I had sweat beading from my brow. I could feel my hair becoming saturated in sweat. My whole body was exhausted, and I really needed to grab some water from the employee lounge.

"A few more boxes," I told myself out loud as I hoisted some of the dry cat food bags over my shoulder and relocated them.

I looked back toward the door. The rain was still coming down, bringing the wrath of God with it. The water was bubbling through steadily. At least the product was going to be ok. I put the mop against the wall, pushing the bucket out of the way after one final pass through to collect standing water. I earned myself water from the work fridge.

I turned and headed for the receiving swinging doors and made my way down the back aisle toward the break room.

"We need a backup cashier at the front. Backup cashier to the front."

I heard the squelch of the phone intercom as the phone was placed back on the receiver. That would be me, I assume. I'm the only other person today other than the manager, and he sure as shit wasn't coming up to cash out people. It's pouring outside, it couldn't be too bad, right? Three, four people, tops. I'll handle that, and head back up here. No biggie.

Fifteen people. Fifteen people requiring checkout. Where the hell did everyone come from? It's the end of the world outside, and you assholes decide you need to buy a new cereal bowl today? A new gardening rake during the monsoon? The hell is wrong with you assholes? I thought these and other thoughts to myself as I passed by everyone's carts.

I settled down at register 2 and turned on the little light. I waved my hand for the next person to come to me. A woman, maybe in her mid-forties, began to head my direction. She had dark brown hair, short and cropped. She wore a very loud sundress, brighter than the damn sun itself. Unlike her bright and cheerful dress, her disposition didn't radiate sunshine.

"It's about goddamn time!" she bellowed out before I could even welcome her to the register or get through the formalities.

She began slamming stuff onto my register area. Various purchases ranging from food to cutlery, hats to hosiery. As I scanned the items and previewed the things to come, I can almost assure you she didn't need to brave the weather to get these things.

"Some weather we're having, right?" I said, trying to break the silence and make human conversation.

Sundress stopped loading items onto the countertop. She looked up at me, then the giant plate glass window behind me, and then back to the cart. She didn't make any reply comment at all. Not so much as a smile. Just a cold, dead stare to the outside.

"So, did you find everything you need?" I asked, as instructed by my training to do at every transaction.

She violently slapped a pizza cutter and knife set onto the countertop from the shopping cart. She ignored me completely.

I continued to scan the small items and placed them in bags. She also appeared to have loaded an outdoor rug into her cart. I finished with the little things and made my way to assist with scanning the rug.

"You are NOT coming over here near me looking like that, mister!" she exclaimed as she looked at me with disdain.

I practically forgot I left my work shirt in the back. I also failed to remember that I had a beautiful sweat ring to accent the dirty white shirt I was wearing.

I reached down and stretched out my shirt to look. "Oh, I am so sorry! I was stocking in the back and rushed up here to help out as best I could. I apolo—"

"Don't. I don't care. Just do your goddamn job," she interrupted, crossing her arms and displaying signs of impatience.

Any attempt to apologize or sympathize was met with attitude. Sundress wasn't having it. Frankly, at this point, neither was I. I decided it was best to shut the hell up and finish scanning her items.

"Can you hurry up, I have a busy day, and I do not have the time to wait for you and your stupidity today."

She was really pushing my buttons. I finished bagging the last of her items and placing the bags back in the shopping cart. I returned back to the register to total her out.

"One hundred and forty eight dollars and seventy-one cents, ma'am," I said, remaining polite as I could.

She audibly huffed out loud. Apparently, even reaching into her stupid purse was a chore for her, and she didn't have the time for that either. I was a little perplexed as she didn't move for her purse. She stood in front of me with her arms crossed.

"Manager. I need to speak to your manager."

She was so matter of fact about it and so cold that it caught me off guard.

"Ok, one moment, please," I replied, hearing the questioning inflex in my own tone.

I paged for the manager to make his way to the front and hung the phone up. Several moments later, he sauntered to the front of the store, clearly not helping my case. He seemed like he was in a hurry to get back to something, as was I. I had already been cashing this lady out for fifteen minutes, and all I wanted was a water. Or a Pepsi. I could have gone for something with carbonation and punch at this point. To hell with water. Pepsi, it was. I could almost taste it.

"Hello ma'am, what seems to be the issue?" the manager asked as he looked at both the customer and me in the eyes.

Her posture and demeanor shifted completely. She turned from absolutely angry and oppressive to a position of helplessness and being oppressed. Total one eighty. That pissed me off. Don't change who you are. Be yourself at all times. I hated fake people. Fake people really pissed me off.

"Well, let's see," she started, sounding exasperated as she began, "I waited in line for almost thirty minutes!"

She's lying.

"After that, this, this... individual strolled up here as if I had all of the time of the day to wait on him," she continued, "I easily waited another ten minutes as he fumbled his way through the cash register that he CLEARLY doesn't know."

Lying, again. Bitch.

Her voice inflections were like needles piercing my skin and wiggling around. They were searching for the vein to strike and goddammit she was doing a good finding it.

"I'm so sorry. I—" the manager began.

"He then showed up looking like this! I forgot to mention that part! Is this how you want your store to look? Disgusting, ugly, and disheveled?" she interrupted.

Ugly? Has she seen a mirror?

"Again, ma'am, I apolo—" he was cut off by her lengthy, overacted sigh, "I apologize for how you feel today. Let me take care of a discount from your purchase today."

She smiled a bit but wiped it away quickly. It was at this point I realized her game. Sundress was going to go off on someone, regardless of who was standing at the checkout. I just happened to be an easy target. I hated people that took advantage of others. This bitch was no different than the rest of that pond scum.

"Ok, so I was able to get your ticket adjusted with an extra few dollars knocked off of the back end. We pulled it down to 92 dollars flat," the manager said as he stepped back away from the register, "I hope everything else goes well for you. Have a great day!"

With that, he turned and removed himself from behind the cash wrap.

"Oh, thank you. You just saved me as a customer because I was likely to not return before you. May Jesus bless your soul, and God smile over your day," Sundress said as she turned back to look at me, her smile turning back into the horrendous scowl.

She stared at me for a few moments. I equally returned a look that matched. She slowly pulled out her purse, revealing a small wallet that housed several credit cards, some from a plethora of different big box stores down to multiple standard VISA cards. She drew out an AMEX that was tucked behind her driver's license card, dropping the license on the counter with the American Express. I grabbed both casually, stared at the ID, then her, then back at the ID before processing.

I moved as slow as possible without being too obvious. I processed her card through the imprinter, wishing the slider would wreck her card as it passed over. I took the imprint and handed her card and ID back. She quickly jammed both into the wallet and shoved it angrily into her purse. Sundress returned to stare blankly at me once again.

"Well, are you going to just look at me like the idiot you are or are you going to help me get my bags to the car?"

I could feel the defeat in my soul as she uttered that phrase. I was so over with this woman. Now I had to hump her groceries to the outside like I was her servant. It's not like I didn't do this for other customers, I just know how she's thinking about the situation. She likely believes I was put here to take care of her. Entitled cunt. I bet her husband just lets her shop until she drops because he's sick of looking at her and hearing her nagging voice.

I proceeded to push Sundress McNasty's shopping cart into the parking lot. She didn't give me any verbal cues as to which direction she was parked. The rain had finally let up enough to be manageable. That was the only positive of this situation.

She handed me her car keys and told me she was the silver Cutlass on the right. I spotted the Oldsmobile just off to the right side, as far as she could possibly park. I know she didn't walk through the rain that far to get to the store now, did she?

"Go on now, I don't have all day!" Sundress screeched from behind me.

I let out an audible, defeated sigh, and pushed the cart onward. The gravel was bouncing the cart everywhere. Once I made it to her car, I jammed the key into the trunk. It didn't turn. This was back in the day when you had about twenty different keys to make the car drive. Nowadays, you just give it a voice command or whatever. Have they made those yet? I tried a new key, and the trunk popped open with a loud *thunk* sound.

As I raised the trunk, it creaked and moaned from the days' weather. She already had a bunch of shit in the trunk. I made do with the space I had and managed to cram all of her belongings into the boot of the car. I carefully closed her trunk, as to not piss her off for 'damaging' her vehicle. I returned back to the front of the store with the shopping cart, only to be greeted by a disgusted look.

"Well, am I supposed to walk through all of this rain to my car?"

I took an obligatory look toward the sky and the surrounding rainfall. It was a light drizzle at best, compared to the monsoon I was combating just an hour or so prior.

"Bring me my car like a gentleman! Is this the type of service you provide here? I'll write a letter to corporate!" Sundress barked as she pointed toward her car.

I swallowed what little self-worth I had and returned to the car. I popped the driver's side, careful not to hit the vehicle to the left. Part of me wanted to take the door and rip it right off and hurl it at her stupid face. Instead, I climbed into the seat, placing the key into the ignition. This was car key number three, by the way. The engine cranked over after a few worrying noises.

I looked around, checking out the car. It was a disgusting mess. There were food containers, empty drink cups, and other assorted garbage. Disgusting. I shuddered at the sight of how horrible this was before throwing the shifter into reverse. It backed out like a charm, and before I knew it, I had coasted up to Sundress, placing the car in park.

"It's about time. Now get out of my car!" she ordered as I reached for the door handle.

I took my time opening the door. I swear, if I could have taken a shit in her backseat, it would have been the least I could have given her. Hell, that might have been an improvement over the car's current condition.

"Give me my goddamn keys and get out of my way!" Sundress shouted as she pushed past me, slamming the door closed. The keys were in the ignition, but what do I know?

She sped away through the parking lot, nearly hitting a family of four headed to the ice cream parlor on the corner as they dodged the rain.

ΔΔΔ

Marge, I hate these kinds of bitches. People like this in general, they get under my skin. The worst ones are usually women. They can get to levels that most of us guys just don't give a shit about. You all get some uppity over the dumbest shit. I've seen jokes about these kinds of women on the internet. They always got the same stupid types of haircuts. I'm part of a few chatrooms where they bitch about this kind of stuff on a regular. Customer service ain't what it used to be, am I right?

ΔΔΔ

Did I mention I have a decent photographic memory? Not only will I forever remember her face, but I'll have a hard time forgetting her car make, model, plate number, as well as her address on her driver's license. Another thing I won't forget was the look on her face when I appeared at her back door at 10 PM the following night, interrupting her LA Law episode.

Her house was adorned with garden gnomes as far as I could see. Par the course for what I expected out of this woman. I imagine she's the one who phones the police when a colored family moves in, or when that gay couple holds hands when they walk the block. Personally, I don't give a good goddamn if you're black, white, blue, or yella. You wanna bang a dude, a chick, whatever. You ain't banging me, and that's that. I'm not a petty guy to hold a grudge about your race or sexual preference.

However, Sundress, who was standing in her doorway horrified as ever, wearing a purple nightie, was just the type. If her eyes could have been any bigger, they'd have fallen right out of her skull. She didn't close the door as she backed away. That's practically an invitation in, right?

I pushed my way into her house. She screamed as I gently closed the door behind me. I'm not sure why she was upset, I just didn't want to let bugs in or the draft. I stepped forward toward her, holding my finger out to quiet her.

"Shh. Shh. What's wrong? Door to door service isn't appreciated, I see."

She backed away further from me, nearly falling over the kitchen island that stuck out to the left of her path.

"What do you want? Money? I'll give you money! All of it!" Sundress screamed with tears in her eyes.

I thought about it for a minute. She made a decent offer. All of the money wasn't a bad idea.

"Cash?" I asked, turning my mouth slightly into a half-smile.

She whipped her hair around as she turned her head frantically to spot her purse. Her expression changed to relief as she saw it draped over the kitchen chair a few feet from her. I let her run over to it and rummage through the wallet.

"Ok, ok. Umm...Oh god. Ok." She whispered under her breath as she rummaged through her shoulder bag.

I leaned back against the stove. I dramatically checked my left arm for the time, even though I didn't wear a watch. I didn't have this kind of time, and she was stalling. I could tell. I could practically smell it.

"It's here. Hold on... Got it!"

She splayed several credit cards onto the table in front of me, to include the AMEX from before. Was she fucking with me?

"Cash."

I remained as calm as possible, given all of the circumstances. She assumed that I was there for some money, and I'd take my leave. Meanwhile, in my head, I'm working out just how she was going to die. I considered the oven behind me. It was electric, so I couldn't gas her out. Knives are overrated. I wanted something new, something different.

"Please, this is it! Take it and go, you creep!" Sundress cried as she threw crumpled up cash onto the kitchen island that separated the two of us.

Now, I'll take the cash, but the name-calling isn't necessary. I didn't call her any names, did I? Now the gloves were off.

"Maybe you should be a bit more respectful of those that serve you before I serve your fucking head on a platter, cunt!" I threw a bit of bass on it to be sure it struck a nerve.

She winced at each word I said. Almost as if each letter, every syllable, was a knife that cut her. Then it hit me. Her head on a platter sounded like a good idea! How the hell am I supposed to pull that off, really? She had a good selection of knives, but I didn't want to resort to that yet.

101

"Please don't hurt me! Just take what you want and go!" Sundress cried as she slumped into the kitchen chair behind her.

I paused for thought. I had started to rent movies at the local Blockbuster Video store down the road from us. Me and Ginger watched a shitload of movies I'd never seen before, which is practically all of em. One stuck out a bit in my brain. Some Jack Nicholson flick, with the hotel. The Shining, I think it was. Some cat named Stephen King, with a hard-on for horror. Something Jack said stuck out, and I wanted to give it a whirl.

"I'm not going to hurt you, lady. I'm just going to bash your fucking brains in!"

The calmness Jack delivered the line mirrored that of my own. Something about being calm about bludgeoning someone was more unsettling to people than the other options. I ran with it.

"Please! Please, please, please, please...please," Sundress said as she slumped over and made her way to the floor from the chair.

I'm not sure what laying on the floor solves. I always saw some stupid shit in the movies me and Ginger watched but never thought it would happen in real life. People checking out noises, going back inside, and falling to the floor. That always drove me nuts. Idiots.

While I commiserated with nostalgic memories of movie night, Sundress took the chance to make a run for it. Her feet found the ground and pushed her along through to the living room. I slowly and calmly followed. Shame I didn't have an ax or a baseball bat for effect. She never fully stood up. That also was annoying. The chase was part of the fun.

Sundress moved through the living room, bumping into all of the furniture along the way. She would let out a squeal with each item behind her as if a coffee table or ugly statue was going to be her demise. I followed slowly at first until she climbed to her feet using a decorative vintage chair from the 1940s for assistance.

Chapter 8

"Please!" She begged once more.

I don't know why she kept asking please. I understood manners. I said I was going to kill her, and she asked, 'please.' When I'm done, I'll be sure to provide a 'thank you' in response. She continued with her pleas of 'please' as she backed around the corner to a large hallway. She stumbled through the threshold of the bathroom and hit her head on the toilet bowl on the way down.

Part of me wanted to kick myself. Did the toilet just take away the satisfaction? Did she get bumped off by the john? Son of a bitch, this is not fair. I knelt close to her to see the damage. It was a big gash on her temple, knocked her lights out. She's still breathing. I was mildly relieved at that, for some reason.

I took the opportunity, while she was knocked out, to remove the shower curtain from the rod. I wrapped her body with it and placed her into the bathtub. She didn't budge. I had plenty of time. Hell, I coulda played a game of chess with myself with how much time I had. She rang her own bell pretty fucking good, to be honest.

I searched the living room, kitchen, and even the laundry room for something inventive and fun to use. I found nothing of value, save for a plethora of knives in the kitchen and Tupperware. Lots and lots of Tupperware. I moved through the rest of the house, checking on the bathroom as I did so.

The bedroom was my last step. Maybe her husband had a baseball bat or a gun or something. I'd have rather preferred not to use the gun, but the bat wouldn't be out of the cards. The bedroom was pristine. The bed was made, curtains were pulled perfectly, and the surfaces were clean and organized. This was absurd. Her car was a shit hole, but this is how she sleeps? I'd ask how she sleeps at night, but I can take a stab at it.

I checked the bureau drawers on either side of the bed. Nothing good, save for a box of condoms for some reason, as well as a few home shopping magazines. I couldn't tell whose was who's based on the contents because frankly, both sides had some strange shit.

I threw open the closet door. I rooted around for anything of interest. It was then that I saw it: a metal coat hanger. One of those heavy-duty thick types. Still bendable, but one that wouldn't snap in half with a heavy coat hung on it. I grabbed it from the clothing rod it hung from with a smile on my face. I had an idea.

I gripped the clothes hanger as I returned back into the bathroom. Sundress was stirring, but not quite back with us yet. This worked out plenty for me, and I went to work.

I stretched the hanger a bit and placed it over her head. I lowered it down to the neck area, letting it rest around her neck. I was about to rig something up, I just needed time. I rushed back out to the kitchen, ripping open all of the drawers. I was looking for a specific item. They had to have a junk drawer. Everyone did.

After about six drawers, I found the treasure. Inside, some clothesline twine, about fifty feet of the stuff. I had to engineer something interesting. I returned back to the bathtub to complete my masterpiece.

Looking around, I only realized now that the curtain rod wasn't one of them glue up pieces of shit. This was the real deal, screwed into the studs. This was made out of solid metal, unlike the cheap shit we sold at work. I put the rope over the top and tied the end tightly onto the back of the hanger.

The other end I spooled out until I had enough of it wrapped around the pole. Several loops around, then I carefully led the string back down. I tied it to her right leg. I don't know where I was getting at, but I was too far into this now to give up. Worst case, I'll gut her and leave. I wanted to make a full thing of this tonight.

I went back out to the kitchen, looking for oil. I found a nice container of cooking Crisco over the stove. I hurried back, squirting all of that over the bathtub, floor, and the walls around the tub. She had just begun to come to. I heard light moaning, as she tried to assess what day it was. I took my leave and waited quietly at the end of the hall, with a perfect view of the tub.

Sundress stood up slowly, not realizing there was a large assortment of string around her, or a greasy mess surrounding where she planted her foot. She reached forward to grip onto the wall, and that is where it went downhill for her.

First, I saw her regain consciousness almost right away as her left hand slid down the wall. She didn't fall entirely to the floor, however, stopping a foot or so from the floor. Her head was saved by the coat hanger rigging I created. It didn't come without its costs, however. The hanger had dug into her throat, crushing her windpipe under her own weight.

As she struggled, her foot would pull the rope more taught, creating more pressure on the neck. I could see blood begin to pool under her chin. I guess it broke the skin! This was exciting! As she flailed, trying to get a grip on some sturdy surface, it only worsened her situation. Once I saw the device was working correctly, I moved on to look for a lovely dish.

I checked through the kitchen for fine China. I found a beautiful jewel lined gold plate, likely meant for Thanksgiving or other important holidays. It seemed like it had no scratches, so I'd assume never used and just for show. I was fixing that today because this was a beautiful dish. I wiped some of the dust off the platter with a dishrag and made my way back to the bathroom.

There was so much blood in the tub and on Sundress from her struggling. I wasn't expecting her to flail like a fish out of water, but I'll take it. I placed the platter on the floor just in front of the tub. Fifty points if her head lands square on the plate. Her fighting became weaker and weaker, and I decided it was time to take my leave.

I grabbed the credit cards, cash, and unlocked the front door. I headed back out the back door, locking it on my way out. I bent the credit cards back and forth a few times and tossed them down a nearby street-side drain.

ΔΔΔ

Turns out, my contraption worked, primitive as it was. When the police were dispatched, they found Ms. Shithead herself, near decapitated. It wasn't quite the end result I was going for, but it didn't seem that she had a fun time, Marge. Can you imagine? It gives me the willies to think about that.

When they questioned her husband, they also had to interview her boyfriend, who found her body. A crime of passion is what they called it; I think. I was passionate about my creative outlet if anything, but I think the cops meant the husband. He supposedly sawed off her head and went out for beers, to leave the boy toy to find her. Of course, she is a cheating bitch. I'd expect nothing less from a lawn gnome owning shithead like her.

Chapter 9

Entry 112

I couldn't complain, ya know? Life was going pretty good. Me and Ginger were going steady. Hell, I even got promoted at my job! I was working my asshole off for what I deserved. I was never considered privileged as a kid. I always hated those little rich bastards, Marge. You know the type; mommy and daddy spoiled them, fast cars, free college. Mooches.

But what are you gonna do, right? Life is funny sometimes. I felt I was doing my best. I did my best. I'll stand by that. I went to school. I served my country. I worked in this garbage industrial complex we call the American Workforce. I did all of the right things. Yet, here we are, right? Maybe the whole killing thing got me where I am today.

It wasn't until the peak of the 90s that I noticed societies' sick obsession with murderers. They were recently coined 'serial killers.' Those guys were some sick bastards. Wearing vagina hats and using nipples for light switches. Really freaky shit, ya know?

ΔΔΔ

Me and Ginger delved deep into the movie scene, as well as the music scene. Our home was full of vinyl records, movie posters from films back in the 70s and 80s. We were avid collectors of cool shit. I even found this show from back in the 80s called Nightrider. That car was dope. I wished I had a talking car, rather than the beater I drove around. At least Ginger had a nice set of wheels.

The two of us watched some slasher flicks from the 80s. Nothing made sense. For starters, these guys lacked any finesse, save for the burned guy who haunted you in your dreams. That guy was my favorite. The rest of these losers would stand there in front of their victims, breathing hard, and wait for them to slip and fall. This guy, Freddy, he was the greatest. He didn't waste time standing there staring, but he absolutely knew how to have a good time.

I realize I'm a little late to the scene, but it's just that the 90s didn't really spawn any classy films. That is, at least, until the later part of the 90s. Some movie hit the scene and changed the game. That movie? Scream. Holy shit! This had everything. Me and Ginger saw it in theaters, and I'd never seen so many people cringe before.

I respected the hell out of this. Turns out, it's made by the same guy who made Freddy, so go figure. That guy knew how to create classy characters. This flick had everything. It was self-aware, which was a nice change of pace from the other movies I'd been watching where they act stupid and pretend that a killer didn't just butcher twenty teenagers in the woods every summer. This movie had laughter and slaughter. I guess they always say you can't have slaughter without laughter. It makes sense now that I'm saying it out loud.

Chapter 9

After the movie, my mind was reeling with new ideas. That gut pushing scene? Gold. A costume to hide your identity might be a nice touch. The other guys wore whatever they felt like wearing by convenience. Hockey Mask, their own burned face, but this guy went to a Halloween Store and grabbed an outfit anyone could find. This became even more convenient because with the movie and its spark in popularity, stores had hundreds of these Ghostface guys costumes. I settled on my idea.

After my work shift one day, I went to one of the stores that sold costumes and Halloween decorations. I browsed for a few items, checked out the graveyard décor, as well as some of these fancy new animatronic deals. They were crazy. Some six-foot-tall Grim Reaper figure that would wave his arms at you. Not bad, but not worth that cost.

I picked over a few different costumes. They had the generic sailor suit, various superheroes, and things of that nature. I thumbed through everything until I saw it, the holy grail I was seeking; Ghostface costume. It was even branded with the movie logo and everything. Jackpot!

I picked up the costume and grabbed a size that would fit me. I also tossed in a few children's costumes, generic decorations, and a 'slutty prisoner' outfit. I just didn't want to be that guy who only buys one costume from a movie and leaves. I carried my purchases up to the counter and dumped it in front of the teenage clerk.

"Somebody's having a fun Halloween, am I right?" She asked.

I looked at my haul. "Sure."

She began scanning my items, realizing I wasn't in the mood to really conversate. I looked around a bit. Not too many patrons of the store, considering it was a few weeks before Halloween.

"Slow day, yeah?" I asked, trying to break the ice from my cold shoulder I gave earlier.

"Usually is on weeknights," the clerk said without looking up.

I put my hands into my bomber jacket pockets awkwardly. I pushed my hands deep inside, practically straightening my arms out.

"You have any plans? Date? Party?" I continued to try to make nice.

The clerk stopped scanning and slightly smiled.

"Well, yeah, actually. This dude is totally throwing this chill party, right? And I'm all like 'gag me with a spoon, I'm not going to Tyler's house,' and they're all like 'Well, we could go to this other party I heard of, and the guy's parents aren't even home!' so, like, I wasn't even—"

I zoned out. She went on and on. I don't know Trevor, or whatever his name was, or the cute guy at the Orange Julius with the abs. I honestly didn't give a shit, but I already came in here like a bull in a China shop, so I decided to play nice.

"Chinese teriyaki or something and I was like 'eew, no' and she was all, 'no way.' Honestly, I wouldn't be able to get into my costume if I ate that," she finally concluded what I believed was one solid breath of hot air.

Somehow she managed to ring everything up without issue during her storytelling. Credit where it's due, I'll tell ya that. She pressed on the total key with her long fingernail adorned pinky finger.

"Seventy-five dollars, and nineteen cents, dude."

Christ, these costumes were expensive. I missed the days of making some bullshit ghost costume out of old stained up bedsheets. Gone are the days of making something in your bedroom and pretending to be a Star War guy. Kids growing up today have it so easy. I passed over the money in cash, exact change.

"I really hope you enjoy your little party thing with Todd," I said as I gathered my bags and receipt.

"Tyler, and like, he's gross. But he has like, a nice house and stuff. Steve's house has like, no parents, and we can get crazy up there, with actual beer and stuff. Joey said he knew a guy!"

Honestly, the clerk lost me about twenty times. Me telling you this story, I probably have the names all fucked up. I usually have a photographic memory, but she was a mile a minute and a bitch to keep track of during conversation. I could barely keep up with where this damn party was. It sounded like a real hoot.

"Ok, like anyway, talk to you later old dude, and enjoy your Halloween!" the clerk said as I stepped away from the counter.

I reflected on the 'old dude' comment she said as I muttered out to the parking lot. I'm not even old. Hell, I hadn't even turned forty yet.

ΔΔΔ

I'm not upset about growing old, Marge. You're what, in your thirties, I'd guess? It's rude to ask a woman her age, I know. But you feel what I'm saying, right? At that time, I wasn't old. Hell, I still don't feel like an old man, talking to you today. It gave me something to think about all night.

ΔΔΔ

I parked my car at the bottom of a hill that sat at the mouth of a cul-de-sac. I wanted to try out this costume. I had already grabbed the phone book and found a nice random address to check out. The second house deep into this little neighborhood nook. I really wanted to do everything I saw in that movie because, frankly, it was interesting. I've been going about all of this in such a boring way. I needed to jazz things up a bit.

I walked toward the house quietly. There was a light or two on, but the house wasn't fully illuminated, which posed as a sign of good fortune for me. I'd never just picked a random target, ya know? Now that I'm thinking about it, I really never did. Shit, I guess I knew my targets. Funny how things like that work out.

Anywho, I went on up to the side of the house. I crouched into some hedges they had neatly trimmed along the right side of the home. They obscured the windows pretty well but seemed to allow enough space to squeeze between them and the side of the building. I peered inside the window. This family had curtains for the windows, which I could see pinned to the side of the window frame for decorative purposes. I had a clear view of the interior of the home.

It was a beautiful home with stucco and pocked ceilings with that popcorn shit. The archways that gave way to the room next door were magnificent. Hardwood floors far as the eye could see. This was indeed a beautiful home. I wanted to meet the person who owned it. I decided to creep onward to the rear of the house.

I quickly ducked down as I saw a body flitter past the window in what I could presume was the kitchen. Once I felt it was safe, I peeked upward once more. The kitchen was even more breathtaking than the family room I just passed by! The tile, cabinets, counters, and even the appliances were all coordinated and, well, beautiful! I had a strong appreciation for this design. I don't know why I never considered myself a homebody. I might talk to Ginger about updating the kitchen when I get home, I remembered telling myself.

I saw another person flitter by. Some girl, maybe late teens, early twenties. She was wearing a pair of sweatpants and a grungy looking hoodie with the local football team's mascot plastered all over the front in college sports fashion. It seemed a little baggy to be her own, so I kept my head down in search of a boyfriend. I might actually get a chance to act out the movie scenes after all.

Right on cue, as if my thoughts were being answered, the boyfriend lit up a cigarette on the back patio. I was inches from him and didn't even realize it. Quite frankly, he scared the shit out of me. Just like the movie, and not a detail less. I moved in to get started. He had some headphones on, listening to some loud music from a portable CD player clipped to his waistband.

I could make out the music as some sort of techno style. I couldn't make out who was playing, but I sure as hell could hear the bassline and the beat. Sounded peppy enough, though. I barely realized that I had pushed the end of the knife into the base of his spine, causing him to collapse. I was too focused on the music. Hell, he didn't even scream. I must have hit something good, to be honest.

I ran through my head what played out on the big screen. He was in a chair or something, right? Then a phone call was made, and that guy knocked everyone off. Ok, I knew the first step was to drop the guy. He twitched and writhed on the ground, gasping for air like a dying fish stuck on the beach. He seemed the football player type, at least. Close enough to the source material.

I found a flimsy plastic lawn chair tucked next to a toolshed a few feet away from where we were standing. I was just lucky this family didn't get into the whole 'motion tracking' light shit. That wouldn't have been good out here, that's for sure. I sat Jock Joey down in the chair. He was a heavy sonofabitch, I can attest to that. Easily a few hundred pounds of muscle.

Once he was secured, I decided to throw on the costume. If I was going to do it, I was going to do it right. Luckily, this thing was so cheap I could stash most of it in my back pocket. The mask was a bit bulky, though, and that was tucked into the waistline of my pants. I caught a glimpse of myself in the patio window, and I looked about as dumb as I could. This costume idea was shit, but I figured I should follow through.

I called the number I wrote down from the phonebook using my cheap phone I purchased the other day. Some prepaid deal. I might have to grab a cell phone of my own; they're quite convenient. I didn't set up the account information at the store with my correct information, so it comes up with a 'wireless caller' on caller ID systems if I call. Trust me, I tested it out.

I dialed the number on the keypad. The green buttons were so brightly lit, it was nearly blinding me from my surroundings. I bet there was a setting to correct that. That was an adventure for another time. I had to get my priorities in order. Boytoy was here slumped over in the chair, still alive but likely wishing he wasn't. I decided to focus on what I was doing and dialed the number I saved from the phonebook.

ΔΔΔ

Amazing where we've gone with technology, isn't it? I remember playing some game with a snake, then shifting to having the ability to throw birds from slingshots at couple-a pigs in full high definition. You probably played that game. Shit, Maggie, there are so many games out for kids these days. I just remember coming from the days of Pong. We were happy with a little light and some paddles that smacked a make-believe ping-pong ball back and forth. Simple times, weren't they?

ΔΔΔ

The number purred with a ring. Then another. On the third ring, I heard an answer.

"Hello?" the female voice asked.

I worked on the voice I'd use the past few hours in the car. I didn't think to get some fancy voice changer like they had in the movie. I moved my tongue, tensed my throat, and went for it.

"I see you," I said as menacingly as I could while being as matter of fact about it.

I saw a figure come out to the kitchen once again. She flashed past the doors, not even noticing her boyfriend guy tied to the chair. Drew seemed unphased. I didn't know her name, but I know the name of the chick that played this role in the flick. I think she was in E.T., too. I'd have to look that up later.

"I said, I see you!"

The phone disconnected. I was greeted by a dead tone, followed by the lights on the keypad brightening up once more.

"Fuck," I muttered out loud.

I opened the phone settings and found the keypad option. I turned the brightness down from the five that it was to a healthy and darker one.

"Christ, blinding me, why don't ya?" I once again spoke into the open air to no one in particular.

I called back once again. After two rings, the third one was interrupted.

"Hello?"

"I said I fucking see you, and I'll kill your boyfriend if you don't talk to me!" I dug deep and even scared myself a bit.

I could see her again through the kitchen windows. Her demeanor was no longer a casual stroll for a late-night snack, but one of paranoia and anxiety. Step one accomplished.

"Where are you? Who are you?" Drew asked frantically.

I decided I'd be dramatic for a moment. I let out a few heavy, unsettling breaths into the phone receiver.

"I want to play with you."

I fished for the things the guys said in Scream. I couldn't remember a damn thing from that movie, but I think I was close enough.

"What do you want to play?" Drew nervously said as she looked around the house harder than ever before.

I stepped out from behind the bushes, and moved toward the boyfriend, still tied up and only slightly struggling with a half effort.

"Do you love your boyfriend?" I asked in the same raspy, creepy voice.

"What? Wait? Who?" she asked, almost losing her fear.

"Your boyfriend. Sports type. Wearing this stupid school jacket."

She paused for a moment as if trying to understand this conversation for a bit.

"That's not my boyfriend. I think you have the wrong number. My cousin is staying with me. His parents are on a business trip," Drew replied, with a half giggle.

"Cousin?" I almost lost my creeper voice.

She flipped on the back-porch light. I practically became a ninja with the way I jumped out of sight, like something out of a kung fu movie. I'd feel that in the morning.

I heard the phone drop. I figured that was enough of that and hung up my end, turning it off as I slipped it into my jeans pocket under the cloak. Drew stepped out on the porch and moved toward her apparent cousin, who was coated in a bit of blood and not looking too well off.

"Oh shit! What happened?" Drew exclaimed as she moved toward his body, still in the chair.

I take it as an error of profiling in my book, but the end result will still be the same. I flipped the script just a bit from the source material, however. I grabbed Drew and pushed the knife gently into her clavicle area. I made sure she saw the costume and felt real fear. I'm not sure if it was the stupid costume or the knife, but her eyes widened larger than any I'd ever seen before. Her cousin groggily tried to get out of the chair but found every attempt useless.

"Just be quiet now, and it will be over soon. I'm not done with you yet," I said as maliciously as I could.

I wanted her to think we were going to different levels with what was about to happen. The fear is what I wanted. It's what motivated me. It gave me the rush I was searching for. At least, that's what I think I was looking for. I was never quite able to home in exactly what makes me want to keep doing this.

My hand over her mouth stifled any sort of screams coming from her lips. At least the costume fabric came in handy to help muffle sounds.

"Shut the fuck up!" I barked out in the same gruff voice while trying to fish my brain for a quirky line from the movie. "I want to see what your insides look like!"

That was the line that struck a nerve. Between those words and the knife now several inches in her skin, I figured I did all I could do. I plunged the knife into her, down to the hilt. Drew dropped to the deck like a sack of flour. Her cousin was still trying to move his head enough to get himself to safety. I realized the rest of his body didn't work anymore. His arms and legs were completely paralyzed.

I couldn't quite handle the fact I paralyzed the kid. I decided to just leave the house and never come back. I made sure I had my phone, knife, and all my other goodies, and shuffled down the hill around the house. I removed my costume under the cover of the darkness of night and tree line.

I balled it all up and threw it into my car seat once I returned to my vehicle. I closed the car door and turned the engine.

"Fuck! Fuck! Fuck!" I slammed on the steering wheel in frustration.

I took a few heavy breaths to calm myself down. Once I was more leveled out, I put the car in drive and drove away from the cul-de-sac.

ΔΔΔ

Peggy, I learned something that day. You know how they say don't try this at home on them TV shows? This was one time where Hollywood magic really shines. Shit doesn't work out like this, Marge. It's never the neatly wrapped Tinseltown package topped with an explosion you never look back at. In real life, shit goes wrong, and quick. Fucking movies, with their theatrics and unrealistic setups.

I ditched the costume and the knife somewhere on the way home. It was a good chunk of road between the house I was at and home. I fucked that one up. Then again, I think if I really did or not. Did I not plan it out enough? Did I plan it too much? Maybe I should watch the stupid movie again, which is precisely what I did the following weekend.

After checking it out, I realized how much this movie was shit. Hollywood magic being force-fed down our throats, and the common public enjoyed it. Hell, even I fell for it. Not a bad flick, but it's not accurate by any means. I swore I'd never be swayed by another stupid movie again.

Chapter 10

Entry 113

What was I to do? I mean, tell me, Marge. I'm a good-looking guy, trying to find his place in the world. Kinda hard when the world was about to end, eh Margaret? That whole Y2K shit was a laugh, looking back at it. Christ, I must have survived at least ten world-ending events at this point. Well, at least that I'm aware of. I always believed the computers would be the end of us. Technology, connection, and of course, that inevitable disconnection.

One thing I learned about people, Midge, is that they are finicky folk. They want to be left alone but also yearn for that human connection. I see the disconnect happen. Kids on their phones. Adults tapping away with their thumbs, rather than talk to grandma. Family is important, Marge. I'm sure you are well aware of that.

I bet you look back at your own life and see where things could have been better. Maybe things could have been different? Should you have picked the red Kool-Aid over the blue? Me? I chose not to drink the Kool-Aid and didn't join the Muppets in their quest for computer domination. People, in general, are garbage.

ΔΔΔ

I recall a time when I just decided to buckle down and get on with my life. I was still running along with Ginger. Can you believe it? We got married! That was a happy time in my life. We didn't have much in the way of family, but the courthouse and the judge were more than plenty for us. I think planning a wedding and spending all of your money just to please a bunch of yuppie pieces of shit is the stupidest thing I've ever seen happen.

Over time, we dedicated a small corner of our house to our obsession with music. We had this beautiful turntable that was vintage from the 70s, and goddamn it was beautiful. In addition to this piece, we had a really fancy new-age compact disk player for the new stuff that had been coming out.

I had got into a few newer tunes, but nothing quite hit hard like the classic tunes. Ginger, however, was always quick to adopt the most modern, angstiest sound she could find on the local radio station. That wasn't my bag, honestly. Give me some old-time rock and roll, as the song says. Something about it just soothes the soul.

I had been working for some stuffy office company for a few years now. I left the Woolworth before its collapse. Such a shame. It was a nice place. This office job was absolute garbage. The only perk to it was that nobody really came into my cubicle to bother me. I could do my work, send off my reports via electronic mail, and punch the clock.

Apparently the routine was enough to get the big wigs to move me to some cushy office job, with a brand-new title. I was the Senior Director of Sales and Support. Basically, I was a glorified

120

help desk. The only difference between me taking phone calls and responding to customer complaints was that I was now responsible for everyone else's customer claims. Talk about absolute bullshit.

I went on about my life. Movie nights with Ginger were always in my top five things to do that wasn't work. Among the other four things I liked to do were gardening, hobbyist wood carving, and collecting music. Oh, I almost forgot the one competing for first place: murder. How could I forget that one?

It took me a while to come to terms with what I was doing. Hell, early on, I would have argued with you that I was merely just doing my Christian duty and saving people or being a hero. I don't know if it was the movie theater kids, the sorority, the couple that was trying to fuck in the back of a Pinto station wagon out on some lover's lane, but I loved it. At the crossroads of one of my many outings, I switched from this primal desire to do it to a conscious decision to do what I did.

I think what reinforced my actions was my desire to be a hero. I saved Blondie from the cucks that tried to molest her at the gas station. I rescued the cat. I avenged my beautiful jacket. I took care of an angry customer. The deeper I went, the more I realized the lack of heroics in my actions. I was ok with it, knowing the truth.

I frequented the library in our neighborhood from time to time for research. I'd get on the internet and search up all of the killers of the past and present. I wasn't so much appalled, but rather fascinated by their actions. The interviews were what blew me away, ya know? I mean, look at what we are doing here. Sitting here, having a meaningful conversation while I pour my heart out and you listen. There are so many people out there that love to hear what was going through a killer's mind.

I've always wondered what they're thinking, too. Are they fucking with us? How much of what they're saying is the truth, and how much is fluffed to throw you off the scent? Do they get their jollies off on telling you a lie about their childhood? It amazes me that most wait until their parents are dead before coming forward about childhood trauma. Pansies, all of em. Gacy, Bundy, Kemper; lame. I've watched the videos. I've viewed the courtroom hearings. That clown guy was a sick fuck, what he did to them boys.

I found the more elaborate ones to be my favorites. Not that I liked what they did to actual people, but rather the levels of creativity a human being will go to disfigure and disgrace another. That Ed Gein guy? Fucking make a lampshade out of vaginas. I asked Jeeves for more information on that shit. I didn't even know the Texas Chainsaw movie was based on that guy. Learn something new every day.

The deeper I went into the rabbit hole, the more I found that people enjoyed these stories. Hell, that's probably why I'm babbling on like a Sunday school teacher with the hottest gossip. I got a great story, and y'all need to hear it. But I digress. I started to piece together that these real-life guys were all being immortalized on the big screen. Here I was, trying to imitate the fake costumed characters when there was more than plenty in the world to copy some fun ideas.

I ended up buying a few books on serial killers from the local bookstore so I wouldn't have to look suspicious every time I jumped on Netscape Navigator to search up the latest slasher. There was a local creperie that I would frequent, where nobody would question me. They made a mean crepe. Some French pancake shit. The owners were always nice to me. Ever had a crepe? Shit is good.

ΔΔΔ

Now Peggy, I don't mean to brag about my past, but I was really fucking good. Hell, I still consider myself to be. I studied criminal law, just like that Bundy fuck. I knew the ins and outs of the gig. I also paid attention to what those guys did to get caught. That's probably why I'm still here today and not drowning in a pool of my own blood trying to run from the coppers.

ΔΔΔ

Chapter 10

Ginger came to me one day and said there was a new movie that came out. She said this one was right up my alley and I'd love it.

"American Psycho!" she shouted excitedly.

The look on my face changed immediately.

"The fuck is that supposed to mean? Saying I'm crazy? I'm a psycho?" I began to defend myself, unsure of what was going on.

Ginger crossed her arms, frustrated.

"No, ass. Although you do get that look in your eye..." she laughed.

ΔΔΔ

I let out a slight snicker but wondered what she meant by that. I have a look in my eye? Do I look like a killer to you, Marge? Don't answer that.

ΔΔΔ

"What's it about?" I casually asked, feigning a slight interest in the movie.

"Oh, it's this guy who works at an office and kills people. Chops em up with a chainsaw!" she giggled.

I began putting away the groceries that we had just gotten into the pantry. I don't know why I was angrily putting noodles and sauce away, but something rubbed me wrong about this whole conversation. Ginger was almost overstepping boundaries.

"Well, I called the theater, and the next showing is at 7! Let's go! It's been a long time since we've seen a flick at the theater."

I hemmed and hawed audibly, but gave in. I grabbed my sweater from the back of the chair and grabbed my glasses. I didn't really need to wear them for day to day business, but I couldn't see a goddamn thing in the movies if we got stuck in the nosebleeds. Ginger clapped her hands gleefully and grabbed her car keys.

We started moving to the driveway of our home, and I walked to the passenger side of her car. She still had 'The Beast,' which was the name of her Chevelle. It was getting a little older now and required more maintenance. Hell, so did I at this point. I loved this car, though, and relished each chance I got to ride in it. For that matter, I found myself in love with the driver of the car just as much.

We headed out to the local burger joint and grabbed some food before hitting the theater. I didn't have an issue with popcorn and candy, but I needed some real food before we sat for this movie.

"You're pretty quiet. Is everything ok with you?" Ginger asked, followed by a long sip of a milkshake.

I shrugged. I really didn't know what to say about how I felt.

"Do you think I'm a murderer? Is that why this movie is my thing?" I asked, trying to not come off too serious about the question.

Ginger swallowed her gulp of milkshake. She decided to respond to me after shoveling a few fries into her mouth.

"No, I'm just saying that you like these slasher movies with me. Honestly, I probably want to see it more than you. You look like you get squeamish around bloody scenes."

I laughed internally at that comment.

"Plus, I don't think you'd hurt a fly! Remember how that orange tabby cat came around and you were plain ol' terrified of him? Treated a cat like you'd seen a ghost."

She had no idea. She'd never know exactly why I was the way I was. Likely, she assumed it was the war that messed me up. She knew I served in the Gulf. Bush didn't have any issues sending us over. We didn't get into specifics, but I just told her I had a desk job. No need to worry her head about the things that happened out there.

"Ok, let's not dwell on this any longer. You ready to see this movie?" Ginger asked as she cleaned up her tray.

I grabbed her hand and stopped her from cleaning up.

"I got it. Head to the car, babe." I said as smooth as I could, trying to normalize myself in the situation.

The drive to the theater was full of loud rock music and singalongs. Queen played as well as some Hall and Oates. The music was calming, at least, even if it was upbeat and peppy. I lost track of the journey and before we knew it, we were pulling up to the theater.

It was a small-town theater, a nice joint. Clean floors and I hoped equally clean popcorn. I'd hate to assume the alternative. The movies back home always had sticky floors, popcorn everywhere you'd least expect to find it. It was a dump. This one cared about their appearance, at least. This one was a chain theater, apparently. Fancy uniforms, corporate branding, and stupid logos adorned the whole building inside and out.

After we grabbed the necessities; popcorn, Coke, and Raisinets, we embarked on our movie journey. We found our seats, about mid-range down the aisle. I still wanted my specs on. I won't bore you with the previews, though. Once the movie started, Ginger latched onto my arm and never let go.

ΔΔΔ

It was a hell of a film, Margie. You seen it? Holy shit, what an actor. That Christian Bale guy? I started watching his other flicks. He's a fucking genius. He played a regular guy at a steady job but was a loose cannon behind the curtain! I respect it.

ΔΔΔ

One scene I sat up for in particular was ingrained in my brain for the remainder of the movie. Bale came out donning a raincoat. Some other guy was in the living room with him. As they talked, he ever so calmly spoke to him about the music that played in the background before brandishing an ax and turning him into puree.

The theatrics. The simplicity. The impact, in more ways than one, might I add. That! That is precisely what I was looking for! I gave up my movie schtick after the Scream fiasco. I swore off it. I didn't want to Texas Halloween Massacre anyone on Friday the 13th. It was behind me. But this was different. This was fresh and realistic.

The movie lost me when he ran through his building in sneakers wielding a chainsaw. That isn't possible. Hollywood bullshit force-fed to the mass market for kicks. But the ax scene was entirely plausible. I had been butchering people without flair the past few years and had been looking for that 'it factor.' I think I found it.

ΔΔΔ

Peggy, we all love a good movie, but nothing took the cake like this one. Shit, I place this above that Star Wars flick. This was pure gold. I only found out recently it was based on a book that was written a while back. I read through that book cover to cover until it was so brittle I needed a second copy. You ever read a book like that? Your boyfriend ever read a book like that? Your husband? Everyone has read a book like that, so don't fucking lie to me.

ΔΔΔ

I could barely sleep that night. Thoughts fluttered through my head about what could be done. The possibilities were endless, I just needed the right person. Even though I barely slept the previous night, I had no issues getting up and going to work. For whatever reason, I had some extra pep in my step. I was all smiles as I headed to my corner office.

126

The snazzy office lacked any sort of view, but I could at least see the outside world. The room was adorned with professional accessories such as a duck-shaped tape dispenser. I saw the irony in having a duck tape dispenser without actually being the brand tape for my everyday purposes. I had a variety of fun letter openers, a bright red stapler that I could spot across the room if someone stole it, as well as a basketball hoop over my trash can.

The desk was covered with stupid things like Zen gardens, Newton cradle, and one of the birds that would dip down to drink. I like to think I was moving up in the world and being the senior director of bullshit and fuckery. I felt like that's all that this job was about. Today was unlike any other, full of reports, tapping away at the computer, board meetings, and the like.

"Got a sec, champ?" a voice said, rapping on my door in an annoying manner.

It was one of the guys who used to share the cubicle wall opposite of mine. He'd always try to show me the latest photos of the ladies he had picked up or list off all of the drinks he had last night to his recollection. An annoying prick. I fucking hated Paul. He was a dickhead, a womanizer, and just an all-around prick. Did I mention I hated this jerkoff?

I raised my head to acknowledge him.

"I wanted to run something by you, slugger," Paul started, "it's gonna be a new way we can handle these open client cases."

I wasn't sure if it was the fact he was always falsely cheery or the fact he called me sports related pet names. I hated being called champ, superstar, MVP, and whatever other sports ball term he pulled out of his ass to belittle me.

"Ok, I'll bite. What do you got, Paul?"

Paul stepped forward and grabbed my armchair that sat across from my desk. I had two guest chairs for the unfortunate circumstance that I'd find myself hosting clients in person. I watched as Paul slouched his body down in the chair until his chin was tucked into his chest awkwardly.

"Let me run this by you, killer," he shot back up in the chair. The level of energy he always had could suck the life back out of me.

I sighed audibly. I wanted to express that I didn't want to hear about this garbage he was about to dump onto my lap.

"I got a new automation system, guy. It's gonna change how we handle the large volume of calls," he sat forward in the chair, "a spreadsheet!"

A spreadsheet? He came in here strutting around like a rooster that fucked the whole henhouse for this? I would have had a better time putting my fingers into a pencil sharpener than to have heard Paul's cockeyed plans.

"A spreadsheet!" Paul repeated once more, just in case I was deaf for a brief moment.

"I heard you, Paul. I know what a spreadsheet is. What are you trying to tell me?" I asked.

He practically leaned onto my desk to get as close as he could. I was more uncomfortable with him the closer he got. I wished he would have stayed in the chair with his chin tucked into his chest, or better yet, back in his hole with his head up his ass. He always shared with me his crazy hair-brained adventures, but this is the first time I ever saw him productive at work.

"Well, I'm gonna take it up to the top floor! I want them to run with this project, and we are gonna be a hit!" Paul announced as he walked out of my office.

I sat there awkwardly, wondering what the hell just happened. Was that a pitch? Was that a way of him asking me for a recommendation?

"A hit!" I heard Paul yell from across the building.

I went back to mindlessly staring at my reports, trying to get going on my job. I typically didn't have an issue doing my job, but something about Paul leeched any give a shit I had inside me. That's what he was, a leech. I carefully pecked at my keys to get through my email.

ΔΔΔ

I wasn't bitter or upset about things changing at work. I never really cared. I always wanted to lay low, Marge. I tried to lay low ever since I worked at that five and dime. I just wanted to mop the floors. I just wanted to do grunt work. Ground-level shit, Maggie. This was just the first job that me keeping my head down and doing my job actually worked the opposite for me. The only perk I took away from it was the larger paycheck it earned me.

It wasn't about the money entirely, Peggy. I had a load of cash stored back at the apartment I checked out ages ago. I kept that landlord paid in cash and probably put her kids through college at this point. She didn't ask questions, and I didn't give any answers. Hell, she didn't even know I only returned there to clean up after one of my nightly outings. It was a nice setup.

I kept that apartment fully furnished. I had a top of the line sound system, a selection of my favorite albums, as well as a few other amenities to make it homely. You'd never know I didn't live there. I always had a water bill due to my showering after I met a new person if you know what I mean. I'd usually play music or use my television while I got ready for my new day.

Ginger never knew that I had this apartment. I'm sure she assumed I handed the key over once we moved into our place. Hell, she didn't even know that I had any money and believed what I did have I made at this soul-sucking job. You know how hard it is to live a double life, Margaret? I'm sure you do.

ΔΔΔ

Paul burst back into my office with more vigor than ever before. I had to do my best to bring my heart back to a reasonable rate before I could muster up a voice in my throat to speak to him.

"The hell is so important that you come jumping in here?" I asked angrily.

"The boss heard me out! They want to use my idea! We are going to be partners, you and me! They want me to be the Junior VP of Sales and Solutions, which is basically what you do!" He paused for effect, "Is that grand or what?"

It was grand. A grand slap in the face, not that I really gave that much of a shit either way. Maybe the fact I had achieved a title and position did change me a little. I almost felt like a cog in the machine of the industry. Almost. I hadn't wholly given myself entirely to the workforce. I had a stash of cash back at the apartment that swayed my thinking from time to time. Although I had that, there was something about moving up in the industrial world that filled in this small hole I had in me that couldn't be filled by my other extracurricular activities.

"It just occurred to me. We never hang out, my guy. Sunday? The game is on, and my fantasy team is ahead right now," Paul started. "Also, my wife hates that I watch it, so can we do your place? You got a TV, right?"

I didn't want this asshole sitting there with me and Ginger. I never really let on that I was married, or that I even had a family. I kept to myself and did my job like I said.

"I have an apartment just outside of the city. It's a hell of a commute, but it's a cozy little place I call home."

"A big-time boss like you owning an apartment? Shock. Anyway, I'll bring the brews if you host the game. Oh, and you should make some buffalo wings. I love wings," Paul said, as he stood up to leave my office.

I always found it surprising how Paul managed to pull off the compliment sandwich. Unfortunately for him, he typically switched things up and insulted, complimented, followed by another insult. What a prick.

ΔΔΔ

Now, Marge, I don't want you to think I was some big shot executive. I was just a standard grunt that was given a high-quality chair to sit in and slave over the same bullshit day to day. Isn't that funny how we can work harder by being given a desk plaque or a window view? The bullshit we strive for boggles my mind.

ΔΔΔ

I cleaned the apartment up nicely. I put away a lot of the random garbage and other things I put out to make it look homely if you peered through the window. I dusted off a few things here or there, but I thankfully kept everything in order. I told Ginger I was on yet another business trip. Perks of being the Vice President of Bullshit, right? Unbeknownst to her, I was only about a forty-minute drive from our house we shared.

I prepared the oven to bake. I set up my deep fryer to begin making the wings. I really hoped Paul didn't mean we were ordering out for wings because I was a halfway decent chef. I knew my way around kitchen tools.

I prepped the wings and tossed them in the grease. They sizzled and hissed as they began to cook before I closed the lid. There was a knock at my door. Paul was here, and he was early. If I tell you 11 AM, I mean it. It's bad enough the game is an afternoon game. I didn't even watch sports either. I went over and let him into my apartment.

"Hey, bro-ski! I got the brewskis!" Paul announced as he held up a case of beer in his hand.

He got what I assume was the cheap stuff. Here I thought Budweiser was the cheaper stuff, but I was mistaken. This was the runoff of what was left after they bottled Bud. How the hell do people drink this stuff?

"Ok, just put the case over there on the breakfast nook. You can load them into the fridge if you want," I instructed Paul, as I pointed to the kitchen.

I made my way to the television and changed the cable box to the game channel. Some guys with headsets at a desk were sitting around, chatting about the games of the past, their hopes for the games today, as well as plans for future games. What a waste of time.

"Want me to beer you?" Paul asked, vigorously shaking an empty beer can in one hand while preparing to sip from the one from his other hand.

I hesitated. I didn't drink alcohol, do drugs, or get into anything these assholes thought was considered a good time. Hell, I didn't even smoke cigarettes.

"Sure."

"Well, don't sound so enthusiastic about it! It's just a beer. It's not going to kill you," Paul said, as he popped the top and walked it to me.

He could have just tossed the can over to me. I didn't like people opening my drinks or handling my food. I usually made my own food. The only person who was allowed to make food for me was Ginger. For whatever reason, I was ok eating out at restaurants with her or having her prepare my food when she did. Strange how love will do that to a man.

Paul sat down hard into my leather couch, his beer spilling from the can as he tried to drink while flopping down.

"Aw, Christ, man. I'm sorry. You got a towel?"

I walked to the kitchen and hurled a kitchen towel at him. He mopped up the small puddle on my sofa, and a bit from the floor. I have had this place for years, and not once did I spill anything. Never did I have anything out of place. Paul shows up for five minutes and wrecks the house.

I sat down in the chair adjacent to him, taking a sip of the piss water he called a beer.

"Man, can you believe they promoted me? I barely do anything around the office. Hell, half the time I'm managing my fantasy team or playing online poker!" Paul asserted, finishing his bragging with a large sip of his beer.

"I'm aware of how much work you do around there, Paul. Congrats, once again," I said, trying not to sound bitter or angry.

Paul raised his beer can to clink with mine in celebration. I hesitated momentarily but gave in shortly after.

"To promotions."

"To promotions!" Paul echoed.

I excused myself to go move the wings around in the fryer. I wanted to make sure they were cooked. I had my Franks Red Hot Sauce ready to pour on these wings in addition to my own additives for flavor.

"Want another beer, Paul?" I yelled out to him as he stared at the pre-game show intently.

He picked up his can and shook it. Paul took a large sip from it, crushing it as he finished.

"E-yup. Beer me, brother!" Paul said as he set the crushed can on my coffee table.

I went into the fridge and grabbed a can, popping the top much like he did with mine. The only difference is I had a little something extra to put into his second beer. Odorless. Tasteless. Effective.

"Here ya go, man," I said as I passed the beer to him.

I walked back to the kitchen to finish what I was doing. I noticed Paul had taken off his shoes and put his feet up on my coffee table, kicking the empty beer can off the table as he did.

"Can I put on some music, Paul?" I asked, walking to my record player.

"Sure! The game doesn't start for a while. Go for it!"

Paul didn't even look up at me. He just sipped long and hard from his beer. I looked through my record collection. I wanted to play something good. I thumbed through album after album. Huey Lewis, Pearl Jam, Heart. None of these were what I wanted to listen to at the moment.

I went into the next crate. Hall and Oates popped up as the third record I flipped through. I picked up Private Eyes and put it on the player, placing the needle at the start.

"Do you like Hall and Oates?" I asked Paul.

"They're ok, I guess. That 80s band, right?" he replied.

I forgot Paul was younger than me by almost a decade. This was old music to him. He likely listened to this stuff in his parent's car while growing up, if at all.

"Well, did you know while everyone refers to this group as 'Hall and Oates', the technical name of the band is 'Daryl Hall and John Oates'? Commonly mislabeled by their last names, which frankly is easier to say than the first and last name basis," I explained with great enthusiasm.

It didn't hit me until I started playing the first track that I've seen this play out before. Now was my chance to take a Mulligan on that Scream fiasco from before. I walked back to the kitchen.

"Beer me while you're in there?" Paul called out.

I prepared him another shitty beer, with a little something extra for flavor just like before. He grabbed the beer and took three large gulps before placing it on the coffee table.

"I should probably eat something. These beers are hitting me, bud," Paul said, as he shook his head dramatically in an attempt to shake off the effects of his beer.

I was going to do it. Fuck it. Christian Bale can take a back seat. I'm not chasing him with a chainsaw in nothing but my New Balance sneakers. I'm going to do him right here in the living room. It wouldn't be the first person I've killed in this place, but the first person I've killed during the day.

I retreated back to my hallway closet to rummage through what I had. Rainboots and a large yellow raincoat. This would be about as good as I could get, I suppose.

ΔΔΔ

Now, Margery, I didn't plan this shit out. I really just wanted to get this guy off my back by watching the game with him. You have to believe me that I didn't plan for this. What I tell you next was spur of the moment and the opposite of what I tried to do with that cul-de-sac fiasco.

ΔΔΔ

I returned back to the living room, wearing a bright yellow raincoat and galoshes. I looked like I was seconds from braving a hurricane outside. 'Private Eyes,' the title track, completed playing. By the time I was back in the living room, the track 'Mano a Mano' was starting.

"Is it raining or something?" Paul slurred as he looked puzzled.

I went back to the kitchen and grabbed two beers. I tossed him one.

"No, Paul. This is my pre-game ritual. I always enjoy wearing my rain gear to ensure that the team I am rooting for always wins. Don't you have rituals, Paul?"

Paul returned a nod of understanding to me as if what I said made sense. What kind of an idiot wears rain gear in the house for their team to win?

"That's awesome, man. I actually wear my lucky socks. Never washed them all season. Hell, I ain't washed them since, uh, two seasons? I dunno. Last playoffs we made."

Paul struggled with his words and thoughts. I saw him wipe at his face a few times and looking around the room in confusion.

"So, Paul, do you want another beer?" I asked cheerfully.

I walked to the kitchen and removed the wings from the grease to drain. I grabbed another beer from the fridge, tossing it to him.

"I'm... I'm good. I thunk I, uh, I shouldn't," Paul slurred harder as everything set in.

I decided to just move on to the next step. I went to get the small hatchet I kept in the linen closet next to a few hunting items for camping, so it didn't seem suspicious. That's how you do it. Don't just buy rope, duct tape, and an ax. That's suspicious. Get camping shit and actually use it once.

I returned with the hatchet. Paul looked mildly concerned but didn't do anything about it. He almost chuckled at me.

"You look ridiculous, bud. I'm still wondering how you're even higher up than me in the company. You're...such a, uh, weirdo. I can't, I can't wait to take your –"

I cut Paul off as I cut him with the hatchet.

"What the hell, man?" Paul said as he grabbed his shoulder I just struck.

The next track began to play on the stereo. I swung a second time, this time hitting his legs.

"Cut it out. Stop i—" Paul tried to say, slurring and stumbling over his own words.

I swung a third time. 'Did it In a Minute' played intensely in the background. I smiled big and wide for Paul as I thrust the bladed end into his chest. Paul slumped over immediately. Just as Hall or Oates, I couldn't tell the difference, hit a high note, Paul gave out. The light in his eyes went away, and he dropped his beer can from his hands.

There was a knock at the door.

"One second!" I yelled out as I looked out among the chaos that filled my living room floor.

I had to think quick. I turned the record player louder, as well as the game. I ran off to the bathroom to ditch the raincoat and hatchet. I felt that was the cleanest room I could throw it into in short notice. I closed the door behind me. I grabbed a throw blanket from the closet on my way out.

I draped the throw blanket over top of Paul's mangled corpse. Jesus, I went to town. I should have put plastic down. Hindsight, right?

"Hello?" a voice came from behind the door.

"Coming!" I yelled out to the stranger at the door.

I skipped over to the door and pulled it open. The pizza delivery boy stepped back in horror.

"Sir, uh, I, uh," he was staggered and stunned with what to say.

"Well, out with it!" I commanded.

The delivery boy recovered and took a breath.

"Sir, what is all over your face? Is that blood?"

I looked at my hands, which were covered in the same fluids. I must have looked insane.

"Hey, no. I was making hot wings, and I got carried away with the Franks. The stupid lid wouldn't come off, and the whole damn thing blew up on me."

The pizza guy gave me his best 'Oh' face as if he got it. He must have because he said he had pizzas for us, for Paul, and handed them over.

Two large pizza boxes were produced from the heat bag zit face carried. The kid seemed so nervous as if he still wasn't sure about this whole wing sauce/blood fiasco.

"So, it's paid for. Thank you," the delivery boy said as he began to turn and leave down the hall.

I began to slowly close the door when it hit me.

"Hey, hang on, bud. Ok?" I announced as I closed the door.

I placed the pizza on the breakfast nook. I washed my hands in the sink and splashed some on my face, returning to the door as I dried myself off with a hand towel.

"You didn't get a decent enough tip, did you?" I asked once I opened the door.

He seemed shy to respond. That's a hell of a question to answer anyway. Who the hell openly says 'Yeah, you prick. You didn't leave me more than a buck!' to someone's face? Nobody would do that. Paul left this kid a fucking dollar. Cheap prick.

I reached into my wallet and presented the kid with a ten-dollar bill.

"Do you need change, sir?" he asked.

I put my hand up dismissively. Smiling, I closed the door once again, only this time to a confused yet delighted delivery boy.

"Must have been some hot sauce mess! Good luck, sir! Enjoy the game!" he called from behind the door.

I stood there, looking into my living room. I smiled a bit at the comment.

Hell of a mess, indeed kid. Hell of a mess.

ΔΔΔ

I cleaned the whole goddamn apartment. I never made such a mess in my life before, Margorie. Leave it to Paul to be an asshole to the bitter end. Luckily the wood floor, leather couch, and few surfaces I touched didn't get stained.

I disposed of Paul little by little. I didn't want to be the guy dragging a rug with a body out to my car. Nor did I want to be the crazy guy on floor three who carried down Tupperware containers full of body parts. I was far cleverer than that.

I checked around town to see any new construction. They were actually building a new children's playground just a block or so from the town square. I found my location. Late on a few nights, I went and dug even deeper than the construction crew dug and put that worthless piece of garbage into a hole where he'd never be found.

They ended up putting a climbing toy directly over top of Paul. They put concrete down, installing one of them fancy new foam grounds to help the kids bounce when they fall off the equipment. Paul was buried forever, along with his bullshit stories and gambling debt.

I'm only telling this, Marge, because I like ya. But I gotta take another one of them leaks, ya know. Drinking this water will do it to you. Nothing but water for me. A healthy body means a healthy mind. Remind me after I'm done to tell you about the time I almost got caught by Ginger.

Chapter 11

Entry 114

O h, where was I? You were supposed to remind me of something. Not sure why you're so fucking worthless, Marge. Oh! Right! The thing with Ginger. I almost forgot that story. That one is worth telling. Trust me, it'll make sense later on.

△△△

I remember it started out typical, you know. Me in the wrong place at the wrong time. Or was it more the wrong place at the right time, or vice versa? I never knew. In either case, I was doing what I was doing. The funny thing was that I never felt bad about it afterward. I didn't feel good about it either. I was just there, in the moment, doing what I was doing.

I did a lot of research. I wanted to know what the fuck made me tick. I'd spend my time at the local library back before the internet really took over. We survived Y2K. The Internet boomed after that. There was a faster speed Internet service available in just about every home. Things were more connected than ever before.

I began to do my research at the house. We decided to get some high tech little Hewlett Packard computer to do some papers on, pay a bill or two, or even play some video games on. I wasn't too keen on the games, but Ginger loved them. I just enjoyed learning all I could.

I remember where I was the day it all came down. It was early in the day still, well before noon. We both had the day off, a luxury we seldom got. The soaps were on TV. Ginger loved that gossip shit, with the who fucked who story playing out daily. I just enjoyed spending the time with her. Her head was resting on my lap, and I ran my fingers through her short red hair. She had one of them super short cuts, which showed off a lot of the tattoos she had on her neck.

This was the only other time I felt balance in my life. I think we know what the other time was. As I sat stroking her scalp with my fingers, the soap clicked over. The news anchors came on. Ginger sat up in confusion because this has never happened before.

"Ladies and gentlemen, we apologize for the interruption. It appears a tragedy has struck New York City. A commercial jetliner appears to have struck one of the Twin Towers. We are patching through live to our New York correspondents who are just now arriving on the scene," the anchor said.

Hell, even I sat up at this point. Who the fuck flies a plane into a building? All those people dead for no reason because some asshole pilots fell asleep at the wheel?

"Thank you for staying with us. As you can see, there is smoke surrounding the site where the plane struck. Hey, can you pan the camera up to see? Let's see if we can zoom in a bit."

The field reporter did his best to describe what was going on. I didn't appear as worried as Ginger had felt. She was sitting on the edge of our sofa as wide-eyed as possible.

"As you can see back at the studio, the plane struck the building moments ago. Rescue crews are en route to save, wait. Are you getting this? Is that a second plane? It's not. Dear God! It has struck the tower! A second plane has struck the tower!"

The excitement through the television set could be felt. Panic and chaos. I remembered this day for multiple reasons. The first reason is apparent; our country was attacked. The second reason is that this was the day that they announced that the Towers themselves fell, and I didn't even get a chance to visit them. Thirdly, once everything settled, they advised you report anything suspicious to authorities. They recommended what to look out for. I fit every description.

ΔΔΔ

Now, Marge, I'm not a goddamn terrorist. I went to the Gulf and shot those assholes in the face. Fuck em. I'm not a bad guy. These assholes planned this shit for years. I'm not patriotic, but I'm not against my country. Don't twist my words here.

ΔΔΔ

Ginger started looking at what I found out was called 'browser history.' I didn't even know the Internet saved everything you did. I only found out she had been looking into these things one day after working a late shift at the office. I was beat. I came home exhausted and wanted nothing but to curl up and go to bed.

"Can we talk?" asked Ginger.

These words greeted me before I walked through the door. I barely had a toe through the threshold before I was cornered.

"Sure, can I sit down first? I'm tired," I said.

She leaned away as I tried to kiss her. Something was wrong.

I set my belongings down and turned to look at her.

"Look. I'm not cheating on you. I'm not stealing our money. I'm not hiding a secret family. I work all day and just want to relax with you," I said passively.

She crossed her arms. I'd never seen her this upset in all the years we'd been together. Honestly, I was scared and nothing really scared me.

"We need to talk about what you've been looking up on our computer. Gacy? Gein? Bundy? Zodiac? Why the fuck are you looking up these people?" Ginger asked sternly.

I didn't know how to respond. Thank God I didn't look up how to bury a body or vivisect a human being. I just looked up other killers. I remained silent.

"Why are you looking up these guys? Explain yourself. This is all you do on our computer," she started, "so I have a right to know."

I hesitated. I didn't know what to say or do. I didn't want to lose her, nor did I want to get rid of her.

"School. It's for school," I responded quickly.

"School?"

"Yeah, I was taking a course back when I got my degree, and I was interested in the topic. Some criminal law courses. These were some of the things that I liked about it and wanted to keep going. It's a passion of mine."

Ginger lowered her tightened arms a bit.

"So, you're looking up these guys. Why?" Ginger asked, less mad, but with concern in her voice.

"I don't know, baby. I just want to know what makes a killer tick. I wanted to get into the head of one," I answered.

She paused before looking to sit down in the chair.

"So, what is it about these guys?" she asked.

I felt a weight lift due to my fast-talking.

"I just wanted to know why they did what they did. How they did it. It's fascinating!" I said with a smile.

Her expression let up a bit.

"I just got worried with all of the movies we had seen that you were obsessive with the real people. I love the killers, and something about them is interesting," Ginger said, showing a slight smirk with that last bit.

I was in the clear. She is interested in it. I just wanted to see if I could talk my way out of trouble, and I accomplished it. Not only was I able to talk myself out of trouble, but I also tiptoed into her curiosity about the subject.

"I have always wondered what it felt like to kill someone. Like, what goes through your mind? What goes through the victim's minds?" She pondered out loud.

"Usually, a twelve-inch blade goes through the victim's minds."

Ginger frowned at my bad joke. I tried to chuckle to laugh off that it was a gag in poor taste. She smiled too.

"It is interesting, though. I'd love to know what it's like to live with one of these psychopaths. Can you imagine?" she asked as

145

she went to the computer to bring up a website I browsed previously.

She skimmed through one of the pages as I watched from behind.

"I don't think I could deal with the guy you looked up that wore women as a suit. The rest of them, heck, I'd never know if they were a killer until it was too late!" Ginger said.

She paused on Bundy's page. I could see Ginger's eyes dart through the text as she read on about his case.

"Hell, you could be a killer, and I'd never know! This guy was the same way!" she added.

I snickered a bit. I don't know if it was the irony, or how matter of fact the truth really was as it sat in front of her.

"Would it excite you if I was a killer? What if I gutted you right here!" I stood up and headed over to her.

Her expression changed as I approached. It was one of mild concern.

"What if I killed dozens of people and enjoyed doing it? What would you do then?"

She remained quiet, growing more concerned. I was now standing right in front of her.

"What if I," I reached down and grabbed her and threw her over my shoulder, "took you to the bedroom and stabbed you over and over?"

I carried her over to our master bedroom and made love for hours. For some reason, she didn't want to walk away from the situation or end our session early. The whole serial killer vibe apparently turned her on. It was easy for me to flip that switch too.

Future sessions, we'd bring knives into the bedroom and get dangerous. I let her cut me a few times, which she seemed to enjoy. It was the first time that my hobby became sexual for me. Likely, this was the first time for her as well, but she was a pro. She enjoyed everything about it.

△△△

Marge, I don't know why she was so into it. Frankly, I think she liked wielding the knife and slicing more than I did. That was a new feeling for me. I could almost let my hair down and be myself; in a manner of speaking of course. I don't quite know what changed in her. Some of the things I looked up say that a severe tragedy being witnessed can alter someone. Others say people are born fucked up and are a ticking timebomb. There's that third group that's been this way the whole time.

Crazy how science works, isn't it? Same with love. These are two things we wish we knew everything about, ain't they? I may not know shit about love, but I do know I loved Ginger. I'd have done anything for her, and she would do anything for me in return. Hell of a relationship.

Chapter 12

Entry 115

You know, I've been enjoying our little sessions, Marge. This has been fun. I got one last one for you. I hope you're going to fasten your seat belt, hold onto your hat, or whatever preparedness steps you take. This one is the best, and I'm saving it for the last one.

△△△

Me and Ginger were happier than ever. Years went by. We were stronger in love than ever before. Something bonded us that no one else had. I respected the hell out of whatever we had going on.

I decided to quit my job. I hated working there, anyhow. I cleaned up and moved out of the apartment. I didn't have a need for it anymore. We maintained our home, but hardly resided there. Ginger and I, we hit the road. We wanted to see everything.

Remember how I said the tragedy of NY changed her? Well, one of the ways was that she wanted to see every goddamn monument that existed before someone destroyed it. We spent damn near five or six years traveling the globe, and eventually getting an RV to tour the United States.

We started our journey on the west coast of the states. I always wanted to see the whole country myself, but I never put forth the effort. We didn't have much in the way of belongings with us, only what we needed. The RV provided a place to sleep when we were in the middle of nowhere.

We went up and down California, Washington, and eventually settled for about a month in Vegas. We played the slots and saw the sites. We loved Sin City for what it was and what we could do while we were there. That was an absolute blast until we had to move on.

We admired the Grand Canyon. We checked out the rolling hills of Montana and braved the cold of Wisconsin and Michigan. I honestly loved the cold places, but Ginger wasn't having them. I could get lost in the snow for hours. Something about an open white field of nothing really soothed my soul.

We would always have to keep moving, though, we had to see the world. We made our way back down through the Midwest, passing through to check out Texas and Arkansas. We decided to hole up in a small town called Texarkana. Hillbilly hybrid central. We spent damn near a year in this small town. This wasn't a bad little spot since it was small enough that we could blend, but not too small that we'd be spotted.

We wouldn't have been spotted, that is, until the incident. I was doing so well laying low, but apparently, Ginger wasn't so good at doing this, given the fact she never had to. It happened one late night in town.

The story goes that she was walking by herself one night with some groceries to bring back to the RV. Some asshat waited in the shadows for her and proceeded to kidnap her. She didn't go into detail about what his intentions were. I let my mind run with that bit. Was he there for money? Rape? What?

She eventually fought him off with pepper spray and the small pocketknife I gave her for a birthday years ago. I woke up that morning to the chatter of the town talking about the kid they found dead tucked behind a dumpster. I was proud of her for defending herself, but we absolutely couldn't stay in this town.

Who knows what happened? We didn't stick around to find out. I'm sure if she explained it was self-defense, Ginger would have been off the hook. In either case, I was proud of her. No woman should have to feel that defenseless on the streets. There are crazies out there.

We traveled the roads in search of something. We weren't sure what. I assumed we'd know when we found it. The long nights in the camper, coupled with stretches of road during the day, were taking their toll on both of us. Shit, I was starting to lose it if we didn't find somewhere to hang our hats for a bit. We traveled up to Maine to try to settle for a few weeks.

We passed by a few towns that sounded promising. We passed by Farmington, Bethel, Castle Rock, and eventually settled in a place south of Bangor. There wasn't nothing wrong with the other places, but it just wasn't our thing. They seemed to fancy for our taste. We needed something more down to earth.

ΔΔΔ

Let me tell you, Marge. We couldn't quite find what we needed. We moved everywhere and saw everything you could possibly see. Ginger deserved so much more in her life than what she was handed. I wanted to give her the world. She was my whole fucking world. I wish I had told her that every single day. Instead, I went about my life working, and bullshit. Treasure what you have, Marge. You always should.

True love is hard to come by. I don't get how people can be with someone they claim to love but are always thinking of being with someone else. It never makes sense. I'm not the kind of person to really fall in love. It doesn't make sense. I didn't deserve to be given half a chance all them years ago. This woman gave me a job, a home, and a family.

ΔΔΔ

We settled on a small farmhouse that overlooked the ocean. This was a nice touch from the city life and rural plains we'd been seeing the past few years. The lovely couple that took us in, John and Martha, were about as sweet as could be.

The couple was a happy little family who clearly loved the rustic life. They raised a small son of their own, they said, who went to work in the big city. Ginger and I were struggling to raise our own while on the road. This was part of the reason we had to find somewhere to settle and fast.

I made myself useful to John on the farm. It wasn't much that was required, but I did everything I could. I'd feed their chickens and pluck the apples from their trees if they needed it. Ginger would always find herself helping Martha with the clothes or other household chores. Even though the couple wasn't but fifteen to twenty years older than we were, they became very quickly like parents to both of us.

Family is a funny thing. It really makes you feel like you belong, ya know? Other times, they're the last people on the planet you want to deal with. I'd do anything for my family. Ginger, my son, hell, even John and Martha. These guys were classy, too, and just as much family.

Martha was getting older and frailer. I could tell that her once beautiful blonde hair turned gray was thinning by the weeks. John wasn't getting any younger either. Thankfully, for his sake, he was built like an ox. I've seen this guy get the flu and continue to move heavy bags of feed for the chickens. He was a trooper.

Months went by, and we stayed for the winter. There was no sense in leaving before a giant storm. Ginger and I wanted to do what we could to help. The storm ended up being what I'd call the Storm of the Century for Maine. This was rough. Snow as far as the eye could see.

Ginger and I decided to trek into town to get a few things. The trucks weren't making it through this snow, but I had two working feet that could. We let John and Martha know we'd be back in a day or so with a few necessities for them.

Ginger and I set out, leaving our son with our adopted grandparents to watch out for him. He always enjoyed John's baseball card collection and wished his own son was as curious about them as ours was. The weather was cold, so we bundled up tight.

ΔΔΔ

Now, we weren't stupid, Midge. We knew better. We knew we were headed into the freezing cold. You ever been somewhere so cold that your dick would fall off from frostbite if you took too long of a piss? That's some cold right there.

ΔΔΔ

We had made it into town without issue. It was late afternoon by the time we got to the stores, and a lot of them were closing down to get home to their own families. It was a ghost town. It's not like this place was populated regularly, but today it was barren. The snow wasn't doing it any favors, either.

"You want to find somewhere to stay the night, and we get the stuff in the morning and head back after?" Ginger asked, looking visibly tired from the journey.

I looked around. Most of the stores had closed. It must have been around four in the afternoon at this point. The sun was already setting. I nodded in agreement with her decision and found a local motel to stay for the night.

The night wasn't uneventful, however. The couple next to us was beating a hole in the wall with the headboard. Must have been a newlywed couple come out here to find a romantic getaway. Only newlyweds fuck that hard and heavy. That was true until I heard the phone ring through the wall.

"Hello?" a woman's voice said from through the plaster.

For whatever reason, Ginger and I were enthralled to eavesdrop. The TV didn't get any signal, and there wasn't much else we could do.

"Oh, you know, work, work, work. How is it back home?" the woman asked.

We continued to listen. We heard a set of footsteps trod off to the far side of the room, presumably to take a piss.

"Oh, the conference? Boring as always. You know I'd rather be home with you. How are the kids?" the voice waited for a moment. "That's good. Well, you give them a kiss from mommy and give yourself one too. I have to go, busy day tomorrow."

The voice became inaudible for a moment. Me and Ginger looked at each other in disgust. This adulteress bitch. We both had the same look across both of our faces. I decided I wanted to go next door and say something about it.

"Don't go over there. It's not your business," Ginger pled as she grabbed my forearm.

The couple next door began to go at it again like rabbits. The banging on the wall resumed.

"You can sleep through that shit?" I asked.

Ginger sighed. I was right. Well, maybe half right. Either way, I was right enough.

Ginger threw on her robe that she grabbed from the closet. I always loved it when places gave nice little robes to their guests. I took the room key, placed it into my sock, and put my boots on over the socks. The key rested just above my ankle, held nice and snug. I didn't put on pants because they were still wet from the snow. They were hanging over the tub.

Ginger put her boots on and clasped her robe. I planned to just go over in my boxers and boots. Really quick, in and out.

The door opened, and the gust of frigid night air burst through. My nipples could have cut diamonds; they were so hard from the cold. I had to brave the weather to go to the next room, however. The two of us set out to have a word with this cheating harlot.

I approached the door and prepared to knock. Before I could, Ginger burst past me and beat on the door heavily. We could hear the couple through the front door, even over the whipping winds. They stopped after Ginger rapped on the door once more. I assumed they were getting themselves presentable.

The door slid open slightly. It was the woman we heard on the phone through the wall.

"Oh shit! I think this is your wife!" she announced as the male in the room pulled the door open from behind her.

Stud seemed relieved that Ginger wasn't his wife. That just upped the ante, though. It made me sick. I was ready to go to my mental place and do what needed to be done, but I had to think about Ginger.

"You cheating pieces of shit are so fucking loud that my husband and I can't get a decent sleep! You disgust me!" Ginger began to rip them apart verbally.

Chapter 12

I was amazed as I followed her slowly into the room while the onslaught of words poured out of her. I was even a little turned on when she pushed the woman down after she tried to approach Ginger. The two of them relegated to the bed, where they sat in shame.

I wandered the room a bit, looking around. It was set up just like ours, just mirrored slightly. They really do cookie-cut these things, don't they? Even in a small town.

As I picked up the Stud's wallet, I heard a familiar noise. The gurgling sound I was so acquainted with. Had I blacked out and woke up to a scene again? That's happened a few times. I don't know if my body was craving the act so hard that I went autopilot or something, but it happened a lot.

I looked over to see my wife, the mother of my children, choking the life out of the woman adulterer. Stud tried his best to pull them apart, but he wasn't having much luck. I decided I'd step in.

I grabbed the alarm clock next to the bed and wrapped the cord around Stud's neck. I pulled back hard and quick. I wasn't looking to black him out. I want to finish this, as I always had in the past. Ginger was so busy with what she was doing, she didn't notice that I was choking the life out of the other person in the room!

As Stud dropped down, slowly giving up the fight, I tightened the cord around his throat even more. I put some elbow into it, crushing his esophagus. He went limp almost immediately. I dropped everything and let him slump onto the bed, landing against the headboard. I glanced over to see what was going on with Ginger and the adulteress.

Ginger apparently brandished her pocket knife I gave her. She withdrew it from the pocket of the robe, which had flown open in the fray. Her beautiful breasts were exposed, as she thrust the knife into the side of the other woman. The two of them threw down and around for a while before they fell down off the side of the bed, crashing to the floor.

Thankfully we were shacked up on the first floor, so no one underneath was alerted. I sat up concerned with what had happened. I wasn't sure if Ginger was ok or not.

"I'm good."

A voice calmly said as a bloody thumbs up thrust up over the edge of the bed.

"Thank God. I got worried," I said as I reached my hand out to help Ginger to her feet.

As she stood, I saw her covered in this woman's blood. Breasts were coated in the red substance, as well as her arms, legs, and face. I stood up to see what the damage was. This was uncleanable. This was a disaster. This was, dare I say it, hot?

I grabbed the body of the dead woman and flung it onto the bed next to her booty call. I figured they should be together, right?

"Now what?" Ginger calmly asked me, with a hint of seduction in her voice.

Was she feeling what I was feeling? This was interesting. This was, well, new.

I grabbed my woman and threw her to the area at the foot of the bed. For at least an hour or two, we made passionate love as the other couple looked on. We had blood smeared on both of us. After we were a sweaty, bloody mess, we decided to clean up in their shower. We stole the robes from their room in exchange for the soiled ones.

ΔΔΔ

Now, Margie, we were like damn jackrabbits. This seemed to be the thing. I never knew she had it in her. I mean, I knew she did the kid in the alley, but this was in front of me. We weren't standing for that adultery bullshit. We were a happy couple, and even more so that we've found something to add to our already burning fire.

I wish more people felt the way we did. I hope more people found whatever could ignite their fire like we did. I'm not saying to do exactly what we did, but find something for you. If it ain't working out, let the significant other know, feel me? That's what pissed me off about the whole situation, and we found a new purpose.

We went back to John and Martha, gave them their supplies, and set off after the first thaw. We decided that being so far up north wasn't for us, and eventually made our way south.

Chapter 13

Margie, Margie, Margie. How I have loved the time we have shared together. This has been a real gift, ya know? Having you around, listening to my stories while we record what will be my opus is fantastic. This is the story as I remember it. And we are creeping toward the end, but I do have one final story. Don't bother moving, because it's not too long.

ΔΔΔ

Me and Ginger had begun moving south. We stopped for a bit in Pennsylvania, eventually making our way further down. The city we stopped in was full of life. It was so vibrant and so crowded. I wish we'd have put more time into that place, but we also knew how to not exceed our welcome.

Chapter 13

We took the RV to a beautiful little place outside the city but resided in a nice hotel within city limits. We were positioned next to the Inner Harbor, a spot the locals hated, yet treasured. I tried to understand precisely what the charm was about this city. The people wore the local teams proudly while eating disgusting seafood.

It was summer by the time we made our way to this place. Ginger and I were looking to stretch our legs a bit and walk the city. We weren't afraid of nothing. When you look at death in the eye as much as we did, it don't mean jack shit.

ΔΔΔ

You know that feeling you get when you're with your soulmate, Marge? That vibe you get when you can just bounce off each other? I love that feeling. I only wish you understood that feeling as much as Ginger and I did.

ΔΔΔ

We saw the sights. We climbed aboard beautiful ships and toured the finest museums. We saw everything the city had to offer. We would walk past the same neighborhoods every day. The brownstones and rowhomes were always beautiful to us.

There was one particular stretch of road we would end up on. It was lined with potted plants and beautiful chalk drawings from the children. We loved walking through that area. Our son, in particular, loved to chat it up with everyone outside. He eventually made friends with some gentleman that would always be found outside, polishing his car.

Shelby seemed like a nice guy. He was close to our age, maybe just a bit older. He probably loved his Ford more than life itself. That was clear with every Saturday morning's routine polish and shine of his Mustang. Ginger, of course, liked it because it was a muscle car. We left the Chevelle garaged back home. Our son had never even seen our house, and we were looking to fix that soon.

ΔΔΔ

You know what it's like to never know you have a home? I felt like that all my life. My daddy ran out on us for another woman when I was little. My momma lost her mind. Ginger didn't have much in the way of family either. We never knew what home was and didn't want that life for our little guy.

ΔΔΔ

One week, we noticed the Mustang hadn't been shined per usual. Shelby was nowhere to be found. This repeated for another week or so until we managed to catch him leaving his house. He was just locking up the door when the three of us approached him.

"Hey, Shel, everything ok buddy?" I asked.

Shelby took a deep breath. He tried his hardest to muster up the courage to speak. Something was weighing on him, I could tell. He took a glance at our kid.

"Hey, sport. Can you go take a look at Mr. Shelby's car for a second? Stay on the sidewalk and count the dirt spots. He's gonna need your help!" I said, trying to task my kid into something.

"It's my wife. She's been running around on me. I just got word today that she's actually not in California, but in fact just down the road. She's been gone for three days. She didn't call me or check-in, but I assumed she was busy," Shelby said, holding back a few tears.

I didn't know what to say. Ginger was quicker on the draw and hugged him.

"I just wish I had what you guys have. I always see you holding hands with your boy and walking the block. You're always cheery and happy. I miss that with me and my old lady," Shelby said as a stream of tears began to escape from his eyes.

ΔΔΔ

We stayed with him long enough to know enough about what was going on. He even knew it was one of his friends, someone from the office where he and his wife worked. They both worked up at the local hospital, in the psychology or psychiatry ward or something. Crazy, right?

Here these people were trained to teach your brain to work right, and they had no idea how to operate their own. When they were hit with adversity, they'd shell up and shut down. Relationship coaching, life advice, and all they preach is absolute shit, Marge. I'm sure you're well aware of that.

△△△

Shelby told us the following weekend that he knew exactly where she was today. She was no longer meeting at work because she felt someone was watching. She met her secret lover just across town, in an empty building. Talk about disgusting, right?

We followed her a few times to see exactly where she went off to. Her flowing brown hair always pulled tight into a professional bun. It was in a bun, that is, until she left the building she spent an hour or two in. When she would exit, she would have her hair down, flowing everywhere. Her clothing would be in disarray. We knew what was going on. We had seen it so many times before.

What the hell are you to do, though? We let Mr. Shelby know all about what his wife was up to, and confirmed we saw her leaving a building in a disheveled state on one of our walks. He vowed he would get her one day. I don't blame him. At this point, I don't know how I'd handle Ginger cheating on me if she did.

Weeks went by. We followed his wife to her various hangouts. She would always do the deed during the day in busy neighborhoods. These neighborhoods helped us blend but didn't help with trying to get closer. We decided to leave our son behind with Mr. Shelby one day.

I know, I know. What a risk, right? But he seemed like he had it together. He didn't look like a killer. Seemed an alright guy to me. Mr. Shelby agreed to watch our kid while we ran errands. I don't know if he knew what errands we were going to run, or if he was oblivious to the whole thing, but we set off.

We followed his wife through the city. She stopped off at various places, as before. It wasn't until she went to the empty neighborhood once more with a gentleman caller, that we knew we had her.

Ginger followed behind closely while I hung back. She was a pro at this point. She bumped into this lady, knocking down an armful of items she was carrying. One of which was a bottle of wine that crashed to the pavement.

"What a shame! I'm so sorry! Excuse me," Ginger said as she helped Shelby's wife pick up her other items.

"It's just wine, I can buy more," she said.

Ginger stood up and shook her hand.

"Let me take care of the bottle for you. Are you almost home? I'd be more than happy to walk you the rest of the way and give you cash."

The woman smiled.

"Sure. You can help me carry a few things, so I don't drop them again. I appreciate it. You're so nice! I'm meeting someone soon, so I have to get there quick. He's expecting wine, but I'll break the news to him," she said. "At least you'll be there to back up the story."

I watched the two of them disappear into a building as I carefully followed. I did my best to keep a distance without losing them. I went through the door and followed them upstairs. This was some older office building of sorts. The décor was dated severely.

I could hear their voices on the floor above me, as a door creaked open. I held my position in the stairwell, waiting for a good signal. I could hear a male voice, my wife, and Shelby's wife. I knew I was in the clear when I heard a loud thud. I moved quickly up the stairs and tried the door. Unlocked.

I whipped open the door to a therapist's office to find my wife standing over an unidentified half-naked man, while Shelby's wife crouched into the corner, screaming frantically.

ΔΔΔ

See Marge. I tell you this only to let you know why you're in this position. You use your power to manipulate and twist your way through life. Mr. Sanchez didn't deserve to be treated the way he was by you. I wanted to give you my whole life story using this equipment you have here as a window into why this is happening.

Do you record your sex sessions on these tapes? Or do you interview people with them? It's a pretty elaborate setup if you ask me. I'm just glad we brought rope and duct tape along for the journey. Never know when you'll need those.

I'm also sorry about your friend here. Ginger isn't too gentle when it comes to the male counterpart. Hell, she isn't too gentle when it comes to ladies either. But you ain't no lady, are ya? You're trash. We're just the garbage folk taking it out.

ΔΔΔ

Tape ends

Author's Note

A s an author, it's fun to get into the mentality of other characters. It gives you a chance to essentially 'become' someone else for a while. The worrisome part is that all of these people are technically a part of you. I wrote a music album some decades ago, sharing the same title. The content of that album was akin to Alice Coopers: "Welcome To My Nightmare." I told a story of a serial killer who had blacked out all of his memories and managed to return to his hometown decades later. He revisits friends and loved ones, or at least tries to, and realizes through each song precisely what he had done. It's a full mental breakdown through twelve songs. I always thought it was a fresh concept.

This time around, I'm telling the story differently. This time, you don't explore the murders after the fact in the same sense. You get them from the perspective of our main attraction. I'm hoping that I can do this story justice as I piece together the story from the old recorded album, transcribing them into an account that will have you on the edge of your seat. Sometimes, I worry myself when I get too deep into a story like this. I frighten myself thinking where these thoughts come from. Is it creativity when writers discuss situations and scenes like this, or something else? To be able to sit down with some of the horror genre greats and ask would be great.

I'm super excited to have shared this story. I hope you enjoyed it.

About The Author

Harry Carpenter was born in 1985, in Baltimore, Maryland. His writing spans comedy to horror, as an avid fan of both. He likes cats, Raisinets, and loves his wife.

Harry has an obsession for twisted horror mixed with humor. His writing reflects both sides of his brain, as they compete for dominance, formulating the dark humor portrayed in his books.

Other Books by Harry Carpenter

Tales From An Ex-Husband

Spooky Tales and Scary Things

Brain Dump: A Poetry Collection

FUBAR: Blackout

Tales From An Ex-Employee

Made in the USA
Middletown, DE
14 August 2020